Acclaim for

'Greek mythology as you have never known it: powerfully integrated within the weft and warp of this fast-moving adventure story' Lindsey Fraser, *Guardian*

'Engaging and well-researched' *Times Educational Supplement*

'Mythology for the Playstation generation' *Armadillo*

'Gallops through Ancient Greece causing a lot of fun' *School Librarian*

'An exciting, fast-paced story [that] cleverly combines magic, ancient Greek legends, science and philosophy' Richard Young, Cambridgeshire Libraries

JOSHUA CROSS

& THE QUEEN'S CONJUROR

DIANE REDMOND

Originally published in 2004 by Wizard Books,
an imprint of Icon Books Ltd.

This edition published in the UK in 2005 by Wizard Books,
an imprint of Icon Books Ltd.,
The Old Dairy, Brook Road, Thriplow, Cambridge SG8 7RG
email: wizard@iconbooks.co.uk
www.iconbooks.co.uk/wizard

Sold in the UK, Europe, South Africa and Asia by
Faber and Faber Ltd., 3 Queen Square, London WC1N 3AU
or their agents

Distributed in the UK, Europe, South Africa and Asia by
TBS Ltd., Frating Distribution Centre, Colchester Road,
Frating Green, Colchester CO7 7DW

Published in Australia in 2005 by Allen & Unwin Pty. Ltd.,
PO Box 8500, 83 Alexander Street, Crows Nest, NSW 2065

Distributed in Canada by Penguin Books Canada,
10 Alcorn Avenue, Suite 300, Toronto, Ontario M4V 3B2

ISBN 1 84046 619 7

Text copyright © 2004 Diane Redmond

The author has asserted her moral rights.

Typeset by Wayzgoose

Printed and bound in the UK
by Mackays of Chatham plc

For Katriona Funston

CONTENTS

PROLOGUE

Joshua can't find a way out of his dream. He's struggling against a cloying billowing darkness that envelops his face and stifles the air in his chest. He can't breathe, he can't move – he can feel the life force draining out of his body. And then a clawed hand with grasping fingers like a bird's talon reaches out for him. It plucks him up and sends him flying into a spiralling void with a burning light at the centre. Sucked into the vortex, Joshua heads towards the light but he has no fear. His father is light itself, the brightest light that was ever created. He reaches out, eager to merge with the light which he knows will bring him peace, but the light suddenly goes as swiftly as the bright circle of day in the shutter lens of a camera. He is once more enveloped in billowing darkness which is dragging him down. In a frenzy of fear Joshua kicks and writhes, twists and turns, but he is as ineffective against the force as a speck of dust in a vacuum cleaner. He is dragged screaming into a yawning hole and darkness covers him over.

1

THE GOLDEN HIND

It's lunchtime opening at Shakespeare's Chippy in Isabella Street, Southwark, on the banks of the swiftly flowing River Thames, and the queue of hungry customers is halfway down the street.

'Steak pudding, chips, peas and gravy,' says the customer at the head of the queue.

'POTATOES, Joshua!' Mrs Cross calls out.

Out in the back room where the food is prepared Joshua picks up the bucket of potatoes he's just put through the chip-chopping machine and carries them in to his mum whose face is hazy behind a cloud of steam issuing from the cooking range.

'Throw them into the chip pan and stand well back – you don't want hot oil splashing onto your jeans,' says Mrs Cross briskly.

As the cold potatoes hit the bubbling oil the air becomes even thicker. Over the loud sizzling of frying chips Joshua hears a familiar voice.

'Fifty-nine bags of chips and a Coke!'

Dido's face emerges from behind the cloud of evaporating steam.

'Come for a walk?' she says.

'Can't you see I'm working?'

'That's OK,' Mrs Cross calls from the end of the range. 'You've done enough for today. Go out with Dido and get a bit of fresh air.'

Joshua gives Dido the thumbs up.

'See you outside in five minutes.'

Dido's waiting for him on the towpath running beside the River Thames, which is presently at high tide. In the bright sunlight the murky waters of the swift-running river ripple like beaten bronze.

'Which way?' she asks.

'Right.'

Right is past the London Eye where queues of tourists jostle good-naturedly against each other as they wait their turn to see London spread out before them like a vast patchwork quilt. Once past the Eye the towpath's less congested until they reach the Globe Theatre where more tourists block their path as they pose for photographs holding cardboard cut-out heads of Shakespeare and Queen Elizabeth I in an enormous red wig. Joshua and Dido turn into a side street, which brings them out on the waterfront where an Elizabethan sailing ship bobs gracefully in a narrow dock.

'The *Golden Hind*,' Dido announces like she owns it.

'Wrong! A *replica* of the *Golden Hind*,' he reminds her.

'*Of course* it's a replica,' Dido replies. 'But that doesn't spoil my dreams of Elizabethan seafarers criss-crossing uncharted seas in search of new territories for their Virgin Queen—'

'Shove it, Dido! You sound like Fingers when he's off on one!'

Their class teacher, officially Mr Wilkinson, has earned himself the unfortunate nickname because of the amount of time he spends picking his large cavernous nose! Dido ignores the insult and carries on in full throttle.

'You've *no* passion, Joshua Cross,' Dido grumbles. 'Wouldn't you like to be an Elizabethan adventurer and risk your life for your beloved queen?'

He vehemently shakes his head.

'Nope! But I *would* break a leg for Arsenal!'

Dido clearly doesn't want to talk about football. She gazes dreamily at the *Golden Hind* bobbing in its dock.

'Imagine Sir Francis Drake sailing around the world for *three years* in a ship as small as this!'

In an attempt to wake his friend from her Elizabethan daydream, Joshua gives Dido a playful push.

'Let's go aboard,' he says.

'We can't – we haven't got a ticket.'

Joshua shrugs.

'We don't always have to play by the rules, you know.'

Joshua pulls Dido towards a group of tourists who are jostling up the gangplank. Their guide waves a group admission ticket and they all file aboard – including

3

Joshua and Dido, who immediately slip below decks. They settle down in a cramped cabin room, which is set with a big oak table and several matching chairs.

'Ouch!' cries Joshua as he bangs his head on the low carved ceiling. 'Francis Drake must've been tiny.'

'Drake would have needed every inch of space for storage – he wouldn't go and waste it on high ceilings and big fancy windows.'

Joshua settles himself in the chair at the head of the table and looks around the room.

'So what would Drake have done in here?'

'Dined with his officers and plotted his route by the stars,' Dido tells him.

'Why bother with the stars when you could use a map?' says Joshua.

'There weren't many maps in Elizabethan times,' replies Dido.

'Rubbish! There are maps in our history books,' Joshua reminds her.

'They weren't accurate. Half the expedition ships that set off to find the northwest passage were destroyed when they took a wrong turning and finished up in the frozen wastes of Alaska!'

Impatient to explore, Joshua leaps to his feet and descends a flight of steep stairs.

'Come and check this out,' he calls from below.

Dido clatters down the stairs to the gun deck where she finds Joshua trying to lift a cannon ball. Hearing the guide's voice he abandons the task and they run down another flight of steps which brings them into the bowels of the ship.

'It's dark,' says Joshua as he looks around trying to get accustomed to the gloom. 'Wonder what they kept down here?'

'Supplies – and rats,' Dido speculates.

There's a scuffling behind which makes them nervously clutch hold of each other.

'Maybe the rats are still here!' whispers Joshua, who's never liked them since one bit his toe in the potato shed.

'Sshhhh!' Dido hisses.

Still clutching each other, they listen to the sound of footsteps walking steadily towards them. Behind the sound is something else ... the gentle swish of fabric sweeping across the floor. Joshua's stomach lurches as his nostrils fill with the rank stench of decaying matter. He quickly looks behind him and to his untold horror he finds himself gazing into the face he fears most. It is gaunt and white and seared with hatred: the eyes which bore into his own are deep and dangerous as a fathomless ocean.

'Forgotten me so quickly, son of Lumaluce?'

Joshua's blood runs cold.

'*Leirtod*!'

Too terrified to move, Joshua stands rooted to the spot. His mouth is dry and his tongue is stuck to his palate.

'I've come to settle the score,' says Leirtod.

Joshua's stomach turns to water as Leirtod reaches

into the folds of his billowing cloak and brings out a jewel-led knife – the very knife that Leirtod had held to Joshua's throat in Hades.

'You thought you were safe,' mocks Leirtod. 'You thought you'd left me to rot on the banks of the River Styx with only Charon the Ferryman for company.' He laughs a hollow laugh devoid of any humour. 'But I have to meet my destiny, which is to kill you in order to revenge myself on your father … and I will have no rest, no sleep, nor peace until I have achieved this end.'

Grinning malevolently, Leirtod presses the flat cold blade against Joshua's pale cheek. 'You look surprised to see me … Ah, shame, did your father not warn you I was coming?'

Joshua gives the truth away by gasping. Leirtod *knows* his father did not warn him! Lumaluce warned him last time of Leirtod's plan to stalk Joshua to the ends of the earth – but not *this* time! What's gone wrong? Could it be that some force is standing between Lumaluce and Leirtod – a force that blocks the whereabouts of his enemy from his father? Sweat springs out on Joshua's brow. Without his father's protection he will surely die!

'I don't intend to chase you through the Underworld this time,' Leirtod continues in a voice thick with loathing. 'I shall do what I set out to do in Ancient Greece and delight in delivering your bleeding heart to your father!'

As the glimmering silver blade slices the air before Joshua's face, the boy finds his voice and screams.

'RUN, DIDO!'

Joshua hurls himself at Leirtod who stumbles and drops the knife. As he gropes on the ground to retrieve it, Joshua jumps on his fingertips.

'AHHH!' bellows Leirtod.

He makes to grab Joshua's skinny legs and yank them from underneath him, but Joshua is running through the gloomy space following the sound of Dido's clattering footsteps. He reaches the almost vertical flight of steps and starts to leap up them, but Leirtod swoops down and grasps Joshua by the hair! Screaming in pain, Joshua twists around and kicks his enemy in the face. Momentarily blinded by the blow, Leirtod releases Joshua who sprints up the stairs two at a time. Gasping for breath, he bursts into the cabin room, where several Japanese tourists and their guide are sitting at the large oak table he and Dido only recently vacated. Dido is waiting for him with eyes as round as blue saucers.

'Joshua! What did you see?'

He gapes at her in utter disbelief.

'Didn't you see *him?*'

'WHO?'

'Leirtod! He was down there!'

She shakes her head.

'I didn't see anything.'

'He's on board – and he's got a knife!'

In a lather of terror, Joshua pushes Dido past the open-mouthed tourists.

'Get onto the gun deck – get into the light!' he yells as Leirtod's swirling black cloak billows out of the hold.

Dido leaps up the next flight of steps and once on deck she sensibly heads for the gangplank, but Joshua runs to the stern of the ship.

Too late he sees his enemy in the crow's nest. His cloak swells out like a black sail as he leaps onto the rigging and swings down to Joshua who crouches in terror. Laughing demonically, Leirtod closes in for the kill.

'HELP!' screams Joshua as he climbs onto the ship's rail. 'HELP!' he yells to the guide who's running towards him.

'Get down, young man!' the guide bellows.

Joshua can't believe that the guide can't see Leirtod who's now trying to wrap his bony fingers around Joshua's throat! Gagging and choking, the boy flings himself sideways and in an act of wild desperation he throws himself overboard into the stinking cold water of the Thames!

Water fills Joshua's lungs but he kicks out and swims up to the surface where he sees Dido wading out towards him. She grabs hold of his sodden sweatshirt and yanks him into the shallows.

'JOSHUA!' she exclaims.

Gasping for breath and with his teeth chattering like castanets, Joshua looks nervously around … but Leirtod's gone.

'He was going to strangle me so I jumped overboard,' he splutters and then his whole body goes into spasms of freezing cold shivers.

'Take my coat,' says Dido as she wraps her pink fleece around his shaking shoulders. He's too cold even to complain about the colour! 'Come on, let's get you home before you catch pneumonia.'

With river water squelching out of his trainers, Joshua hurries along the bustling towpath shaking in every limb.

'Couldn't you hear him down there in the hold?' Joshua asks Dido in disbelief.

'I could hear footsteps and a swishing sound on the floor, but I couldn't see anything,' she replies.

'So you didn't see the knife either?' Joshua cries.

Dido stops on the path and faces the trembling boy.

'Joshua, he's not looking for me – he's looking for *you*. Why would he show himself to me?'

Joshua's skinny shoulders slump in despair.

'I'm so scared, Dido,' he says in a voice that is thin with fear.

Dido vividly remembers the monstrous Leirtod who chased them around the moving London Eye. It was the most terrifying moment of her life and she's grateful she's not seen the black-cloaked demon again, but her heart aches for Joshua who is haunted by him.

'He's come back to kill me,' Joshua whispers.

'Why would he want to kill *you*?'

'He's my father's enemy and he intends to revenge

himself by taking my life. He tried before but he didn't succeed. So now he's back to finish the job.'

'You told me your father was dead,' Dido replies in a puzzled voice. 'How can a dead man have enemies?'

Joshua shuffles in his squelching trainers. How can he tell her that Lumaluce is an immortal who lives in the Fields of Joy with other great legendary heroes?

'My father's a bit, er ... special,' he answers awkwardly.

'Isn't that what everybody says about their father?'

'You don't, Dido,' Joshua points out.

'That's because I haven't got a father,' she reminds him. 'Come on, Joshua,' she urges. 'Tell me more about him.'

Joshua's eyes brim with tears. It almost hurts to talk about the father he loves so much.

'He's called Lumaluce, which mean the brightest light. He's immortal and he lives with the legends.'

'You're not teasing me, are you ... ?' she asks nervously.

'I'm not winding you up, Dido,' he replies in earnest. 'You might not believe me – but it is the truth.'

Joshua looks at her with silvery-grey eyes that are huge with fear.

'Last time Lumaluce warned me about Leirtod, he came to me in my dreams and told me his enemy was coming to get me. He said he would send me back in time to a safe place where I could hide in the centuries.'

'Where did you go?' she asks incredulously.

'Ancient Greece.'

'B-b-but you never went away – you were *always* here,' she splutters in disbelief.

'My body was here but my soul was in hiding.'

'And you came back … which means your father's plan worked. Leirtod never got you?'

'I beat him!' Joshua tells her proudly. 'Lumaluce and I beat the evil one.'

Dido's face is creased with confusion.

'I'm trying hard to understand, Joshua, but if I'm honest … I really don't.'

Joshua throws up his hands in a gesture of sheer frustration.

'And do you know what?' he shouts out. 'Neither do I!'

By the time Joshua reaches Shakespeare's Chippy he's almost blue with cold. He says a hasty goodbye to Dido, then dashes upstairs to run a hot bath. Lying in the bubbly water, he thinks about the last time he saw Leirtod. It was in the Underworld on the banks of the River Styx where he nearly succeeded in annihilating Joshua. The Furies chased Leirtod away but he vowed he'd return – and now he has. Even though Joshua's lying in hot water, goose pimples pop out on his skin and he shivers as if somebody has just walked over his grave.

'With every passing year of your boyhood your strength will grow until finally you will surpass Leirtod's evil forces.'

Lumaluce's words spoken to him in the Underworld

11

gave him strength at the time but now Joshua is scared. He's alone … and evil has come back to haunt him.

The next day Joshua has a dentist's appointment after school. His mum is working in the chip shop so Joshua asks Dido to keep him company.

'I'm scared of the dentist,' he admits.

In the waiting room at St Thomas's Hospital Joshua's nerves are not helped by Dido's graphic descriptions of how Elizabethan physicians yanked out teeth with iron pliers the size of garden shears!

'Shut up,' he implores, but she's unstoppable.

'And they didn't have anaesthetics either. Just a swig of brandy then open wide. Sometimes it took two men to hold the patient down. I read about a woman who dropped dead in the dentist's chair,' she adds gorily. 'She died of shock!'

It's almost a relief when the dentist calls Joshua into the surgery where he lies back in the reclining chair and immediately notices a big mirror on the ceiling.

'It amuses the children,' the dentist explains. 'It gives them something to look at while I'm examining their teeth. Let's have a look inside,' he says, going into professional mode.

Joshua closes his eyes and allows the dentist to probe around inside his mouth with his metal instruments. When the dentist finds a craggy lump of scale on the back of his tooth Joshua wriggles as he tries to dislodge it.

'Look into the mirror and think of something else,' the dentist suggests.

Joshua looks into the mirror. At first sight it seems completely clear but then it suddenly starts to churn as if it were a glass full of crystals. As the intrusive scratching and scraping increases Joshua stares even harder into the mirror where an image is slowly taking shape ... It grows and fills the lens, then floats out like a dark storm cloud and enters the body of the dentist. The dentist's cheerful face twists and contorts and then he is gone, to be replaced by Leirtod's gaunt malevolent image. Clasping a spiked metal instrument, he bends over Joshua and jabs his tongue with a sharp hook.

'This won't take a minute,' he laughs vindictively.

AHH!' Joshua screams, but he can't move.

He's blocked in the chair by Leirtod, who's now coming at him with a whirring drill! The noise shrieks in Joshua's ears and he flails his arms in the air and kicks out in terror.

'NO!' he yells, and grabbing the tray of dental instruments he hurls them into the face of his enemy and runs out of the room.

Dido springs to her feet as Joshua bursts into the waiting room looking like a thing possessed. She chases after him as he races down the hospital corridor and out onto the forecourt.

'JOSHUA – STOP!' she yells.

But he keeps on going ... over Waterloo Bridge and along the Embankment where he finally runs out of breath and throws himself down onto a wrought iron bench by the River Thames.

'What's got into you?' Dido demands angrily.

'He came back,' Joshua splutters. 'Leirtod was in the dentist's surgery – jabbing my mouth with a metal spike!'

Dido hunkers down beside him.

'Joshua, if your dad's as great a hero as you say he is why doesn't he do something to help you?'

The boy shakes his head in tearful bewilderment.

'I don't know, Dido! It's as if Lumaluce can't communicate with me, as if some force is blocking him from the knowledge of Leirtod's return …' He turns to Dido with a face that has turned sheet-white with fear. 'Without my father's protection I'll surely die.'

Dido insists on walking Joshua home. On the way he talks continually about Lumaluce and she listens with her eyeballs virtually bugging out of her head.

'Leirtod was Lumaluce's teacher,' Joshua explains. 'He gave my father great knowledge but then Leirtod grew jealous of Lumaluce's greatness and tried to destroy him.'

Dido stops dead in her tracks.

'Joshua! It's just like Lucifer! Don't you remember reading about the Devil in RE?'

Joshua shrugs.

'I remember, but I never made the connection with Leirtod,' he admits.

'Lucifer wanted to be greater than God – just like Leirtod wanted to be greater than your father. The angels threw Lucifer out of heaven into hell. They cast him out because he could no longer live in the light ... so he slunk in the shadowy world of the half dead.'

'*Just* like Leirtod,' gasps Joshua as he sees the terrifying similarity. 'He's been waiting for centuries to avenge himself on Lumaluce.'

'And now he's found you, he can,' Dido adds grimly.

2

THE FIERY TRIGONS

He's in the dream again. Struggling against a cloying billowing darkness that envelops his face and stifles the air in his chest. He can't breathe, he can't move – he can feel the life force draining out of his body. And then the clawed hand with grasping fingers like a bird's talon reaches out for him. It plucks him up and sends him flying into a spiralling void with a burning light at the centre. Sucked into the vortex, Joshua heads towards the light, but he has no fear. His father is light itself, the brightest light that was ever created. He reaches out, eager to merge with the light which he knows will bring him peace. But the light suddenly goes, as swiftly as the bright circle of day in the shutter lens of a camera. He is once more enveloped in billowing darkness which is dragging him down. In a frenzy of fear Joshua kicks and writhes, twists and turns, but he is as ineffective against the force as a speck of dust in a vacuum cleaner. He is dragged screaming into a yawning hole and darkness covers him over.

Joshua wakes up in a lather of sweat, with his duvet wrapped around his head and shoulders. His legs flail against the mattress as he tries to free himself of the monstrous dream. The dawn light breaking soothes him and he begins to breathe more easily. He gets up and goes to his open window where the cool air washes over him. It was a dream, just a dream, he tells himself. But it's always the same dream. What does it mean?

Joshua leans on the windowsill and sucks in the fresh air. The sun is rising over the River Thames, gilding the grubby seagulls padding along the mud banks in a rosy glow. The steady rhythm of the chugging barges is broken by the scream of a siren. A police launch hurtles by, causing waves to bounce up and splash against all other craft in its flight path. Joshua strains forward so that he can feel the rising sun warm on his face. The light drenches him, then a cloud covers the sun – the sky turns grey and the warmth is gone.

Joshua shivers and quickly closes the window. He snuggles down under his duvet, but not to sleep. The cloud obscuring the sun helps him to understand his dream. He knows the light in his dream is Lumaluce but every time Joshua gets close to him darkness obscures his view and Joshua is dragged away. Since Leirtod's return Joshua has been wondering why his father hasn't sent him a warning. What if Lumaluce is trying to get through to him but can't! Could it be that Leirtod's darker forces of evil are blocking Lumaluce, denying him access to his son? A horrifying realisation dawns on Joshua.

'I'm on my own!'

But he's not powerful or strong, he can't perform magic – and he can't disappear and reappear at a whim!

The shrill ringing of his mother's alarm clock going off makes Joshua jump sky-high. Unable to stay in bed a second longer, he gets dressed in his school uniform and hurries downstairs to help his mum in the shop.

'You're up early,' she says blearily.

'I couldn't sleep,' he replies. 'I was dreaming about dad ...'

He looks at her as he leaves the sentence hanging. Mrs Cross smiles tenderly at her youngest son.

'Funny ... I dreamt about him too. He was standing in a bright shaft of light and he was holding you, as a baby in his arms. He was kissing your head and smiling and then a dark cloud covered him over and you were both gone.' She shudders as if somebody has walked over her grave. 'It was a horrible dream,' she says and briskly grabs a broom as if to sweep away the memory of the dream.

With a heart full of foreboding, Joshua fills a bucket with hot, soapy water and starts to clean down the counter top, smeared with salt and vinegar and little scraps of chips. The steady washing and wiping in the easy companionship of his mother calms him and he briefly stops worrying about Leirtod. It's only when the postman knocks on the shop door that Joshua realises what time it is and that he's not had any breakfast.

'You can't go to school without something to eat,' insists Mrs Cross.

Joshua grabs his school bag and a banana and hurries towards the door.

'See you later, mum!'

'Bye, love,' she calls after him.

When Joshua gets to school, he's surprised to find his friends Stevie and Dido in Elizabethan costume. Stevie points at Joshua's school uniform and bursts out laughing.

'Have you forgotten what day it is?'

Joshua shakes his head.

'It's Monday. Double maths, double science, double games and double art.'

Dido, who's wearing an elaborately embroidered long silk dress with a big white ruff that sticks up high all around her neck, tells Joshua that Fingers is taking them on a class outing to Hampton Court that day.

'That's why we're done up in doublet and hose,' jokes Stevie.

'What am I going to do?' flaps Joshua as a bus pulls up outside the school gates and Fingers appears looking like a bald, thin version of Henry VIII!

'You can wear my PE kit!' says Dido.

She and Stevie usher Joshua into the cloakroom where in five minutes they transform him into a very odd looking Tudor boy.

'I feel stupid!' grumbles Joshua.

'You look it!' sniggers Stevie as he points at Dido's red

tracksuit bottoms that have been rolled up to form baggy shorts under which Joshua wears her long black PE socks, which keep dropping down his skinny legs. Joshua secures them with some elastic bands that Dido gives him, then they hurry onto the bus where Joshua sits down as quickly as he can so nobody will see what he's wearing!

As the bus bowls along the Embankment, Fingers stands up to address them. After having a good delve up his left nostril, he talks about the Elizabethan delights that await them at Hampton Court.

'Here we go,' says Stevie as he smothers a yawn. 'If he tells me one more time about Francis Drake and the Spanish Armada I'll scream!'

Stevie leans back in his seat and closes his mind and ears to the Elizabethans, but Dido eagerly leans forward to catch what Fingers is saying. She's not a conventionally pretty girl but she's unusual looking. Tall for her eleven years, she's strongly built with a mass of long curly red-gold hair that gleams like copper in the sunshine. She has pale skin which goes a warm freckly brown in the summer, but the most stunning thing about Dido is her eyes. Basically they're blue, but the shade of blue varies depending on her mood. When she's troubled or upset her eyes are a grey-blue, like a stormy sea. When she's fired up about something her eyes are vivid blue and sparkle with energy. When she's dreamy her eyes turn pale blue, like the sky on a summer's day. Joshua always knows how Dido's feeling by just looking into her eyes.

He smiles as Dido pesters Fingers by asking him complicated questions.

'Which was Henry VIII's favourite palace, sir? Was it Hampton Court, Greenwich, Nonsuch or the Palace of Whitehall?'

'Really Dido – how would *I* know?' Fingers exclaims.

'Well, you are a teacher, sir!' laughs Dido.

When they arrive at Hampton Court the class forms a long line and, led by Fingers, they enter a large court where he points out a clock tower which shows the high tides at London Bridge.

'Why would anybody be interested in checking out the times of the high tides?' asks Stevie.

'You *definitely* would if you regularly rowed the Queen up and down the Thames from Hampton Court to the Palace of Whitehall,' Dido tells him.

'I thought Elizabethans galloped around on horses or walked barefoot through filthy streets deep in—'

Fingers stops Stevie before he gets too graphic.

'They rode on horses, donkeys and ponies, and they walked too. But it was much quicker to travel by water, especially with a heavy load. The Thames was a busy thoroughfare in Elizabeth I's time.'

They wander into the Great Hall where, Fingers tells them, the court gathered to wait on Elizabeth's favours and petition her Privy Council. In the royal chapel Fingers tells them Henry VIII knelt for hours, praying for guidance when he became head of the Church of England. In the Tudor kitchens the assistants are dressed as servants. They hurry back and forth with trays of pewter goblets brimming with sweet mead and wooden trenchers stacked with slabs of newly baked barley bread. The smell of chicken roasting on a turning spigot over the fire makes them all hungry, but not for them a hearty Elizabethan feast. Instead it's a packed lunch in the sunken garden then off for a run round Hampton Court Maze.

'You've got half an hour,' Finger calls out. 'Then we'll regroup and go back into the palace where we'll be given a private tour of the royal apartments.'

'And no doubt the stinky garderobe where we'll all have to admire the Elizabethan toilets!' chuckles Stevie.

'Don't get lost in the maze,' Fingers yells over their chattering. 'I want everybody back at Anne Boleyn's Gate by two o'clock.'

The minute they enter the maze they all split up.

'I'll go left and you go right and we'll meet up at the middle,' Dido suggests.

'OK,' says Joshua, and without a backward glance he runs off down the path.

'Bet I'm there before you!' Dido calls from the other side of the privet hedge.

Quickening his pace, Joshua winds his way round and round. When he stops to get his bearings, he notices that the path is less well trodden and narrower than the one he's just left. He looks around … there's nobody in sight. He listens … not a sound, not even the sound of echoing laughter.

'Dido?' he calls out.

But there's no reply.

He goes on his way. Round and round, in and out, up and down, and all the time the hedge gets thicker and pricklier so that he has to push and struggle to make any advance. The patch of blue sky overhead gets smaller and smaller as he becomes more ensnared in the maze. Then mercifully he stumbles out into a crossroads where three paths converge. No way is he going back the way he came, but which of the two before him is the better?

'DIDO! STEVIE!' he yells at the top of his voice.

Again no reply. Not even the sound of running feet. With a deep breath he decides to take the left-hand path because it's wider than the right-hand one. Within minutes Joshua realises he's made the wrong decision. It's even more impenetrable than the path he's just left!

As he pushes against the overgrown foliage he hears a swish behind him. He tenses and holds his breath. Swish … swish … swish. The sound is getting closer! The smell of rank decay assails Joshua's nostrils and he knows *exactly* who's behind him. He gags and falls to his knees, which seem to have turned to jelly. Gripped by privet hedges on either side, Joshua hears his enemy's steady advance. He gropes at the base of the hedge on his right, clawing at it with his bare hands. As the cloying smell of Leirtod's fetid breath descends in a cloud around him, Joshua frantically rips at the lowest branches and makes a hole big enough to squeeze his skinny body through. Just as he's about to clear it, Leirtod's hand seizes hold of Joshua's ankle and holds it in an iron grip.

'Not so quick, Joshua Cross!'

Without a moment's hesitation Joshua bends down and bites Leirtod's hand. He bites down hard, until he feels bone and draws blood.

'Agghhhh!' screams Leirtod, and immediately releases his hold.

Sweating in terror, Joshua scrambles on his hands and knees along the narrow prickly pathway with Leirtod on the other side of the hedge, shouting and cursing.

'You cannot hide from me – I will have you, boy,' he screams in fury. 'I will have YOU!'

To Joshua's unspeakable relief, the path opens out onto another crossroads, a clearing where he can stand up and catch his breath.

'Oh, God!' he prays as he stares at the network of paths criss-crossing before him. 'WHICH way?'

As Joshua dithers, Leirtod leaps out and grabs him by his thick white-blond hair.

'For one so small you are difficult to catch!' he sneers as he drags the boy kicking and screaming. 'Stay still, you worm,' yells Leirtod as Joshua wriggles and writhes in his grip. 'Your miserable suffering will very soon be over.'

Joshua's guts melt in fear as Leirtod flourishes his silver dagger. He's trapped! Raising his silvery-grey eyes heavenwards, Joshua prays his last.

'Lumaluce! Help me!'

As the knife descends in an arc of flashing silver, the hedgerow which Joshua is thrust against miraculously gives way and he tumbles over backwards. Leirtod also takes a tumble, but he lands on his side.

'Aaghh!' he bellows as he clutches his leg, which is running with blood.

Joshua can't believe his luck – the demon Leirtod has landed on his own knife! Unfortunately it's not pierced his wicked heart, but from the blood pumping out it's certainly wounded him.

Joshua takes to his heels and runs like he's never run before. Crazed with fear, he runs in and out and up and down the maze, round and round, desperate to put as much distance between himself and Leirtod as he possibly can. He's running so fast he hardly realises he's come out of the maze. In blind terror he keeps running, but now he's confused, disorientated by the light and space. Like a crazed animal that's being hunted to earth, he daren't slow down but runs on unaware of his surroundings. Too late he sees the great barrel of a tree coming up to meet him. Joshua hits the huge oak head on and, dazed by the impact, drops senseless to the ground.

He wakes to the strident call of a peacock.

'Awwwwww!'

Joshua rolls over and groans as his bruised ribs touch the ground.

'Oww!' he cries out.

The peacock's giant iridescent tail quivers indignantly before the bird struts off with an offended look in his beady eye. Winded and sore, Joshua staggers to his feet and sees an imposing man glaring at him. He's elaborately dressed in a flowing red velvet coat with a starched white ruff around his neck. On his head is a close-fitting black skullcap, which contrasts vividly with his long white pointed beard. Even odder, the man's sitting before a wooden table in the middle of an immaculately kept lawn with the latticed windows of Hampton Court Palace thrown open behind him.

'What do you want, boy?' the man asks in a deep, grave voice.

Limping from the swelling bruise on his knee, Joshua nervously approaches the table.

'Er, excuse me,' he mumbles self-consciously. 'I was wondering if you'd seen my friend Dido?'

'What is her ascendant star?'

Joshua shrugs. 'I've no idea.'

'Then I can't find her.'

'She's tall with pale skin and long red hair,' Joshua quickly adds.

The tall man visibly starts.

'That description best becomes our gracious sovereign, Queen Elizabeth.'

'Dido doesn't look like the Queen!' Joshua laughs. 'The Queen's small and dumpy.'

The man turns to see if anybody might have overheard Joshua's words.

'You could be hung, drawn and quartered for such treacherously foul words, boy!' he whispers nervously.

'I only said the Queen was dumpy,' Joshua protests. 'It happens when you get to seventy,' he adds as a polite afterthought.

The man throws up his arms in alarm.

'Prithee, do not repeat yourself! Our sovereign lady is fairer by far than Venus herself.'

Keen to return to the subject of Dido, Joshua says, 'Have you seen anybody come out of the maze?'

The man turns his attention to a thick book elaborately bound in black and gold leather which lies open on the table beside a glass dome.

'No,' he answers impatiently. 'Go seek her and begone!'

'Er … it's not that simple, sir,' Joshua tells him. 'You see, there's somebody else in the maze. Somebody really *really* wicked.'

The man looks into Joshua's silvery-grey eyes and thoughtfully strokes his beard.

'What is your name and date of birth?' he demands.

'I'm Joshua Alexander Cross. I was born in London on the 21st of June.'

'An auspicious date. A fusion of the elemental spheres when spring gives way to summer and the sun is at its zenith,' the man replies as he flicks through his book, which Joshua can see is engraved with all manner of signs and symbols.

'What was the time of your birth?' the man enquires.

'Midnight,' Joshua replies.

'Ah … the witching hour,' the man mutters. 'And the year of your birth?'

'1991.'

The man's head jerks up and his dark eyes flash angrily from underneath his shaggy eyebrows.

'Do not jest.'

'I'm not, er …' Joshua stumbles over the strange word, '… jesting.'

'Are you a numskull?' the man asks. 'Do you mean *1591*?'

'No. *1991*.'

'If you want my assistance you must speak plainly, sir.'

Joshua doesn't know how to be *more* plain.

'1991 is the year I was born,' he says with added emphasis.

'Nay. That is *five hundred years* hence!'

Joshua's blood runs cold and his skin starts to crawl in fear. He grabs the edge of the table to support himself before his legs give way beneath him. He *can't* be in Elizabethan England!

Seeing the boy's white face and anguished eyes, the man offers Joshua his chair.

'Be seated,' he says in a voice that's now gentle with concern. 'Lay your right hand on my shewing stone and let me unravel this mystery.'

Joshua does as he's told. He places his trembling hand on the large crystal dome which is set on a wooden base marked out with the twelve signs of the zodiac. Under the warmth of his fingers a pulse of light begins to glow and crystals rise and swirl in the stone, forming a milky grey mist which slowly settles to reveal an image that Joshua immediately recognises.

'Father!' he cries.

It is Lumaluce as he was the last time Joshua saw him – dressed in a short white tunic with a sword in a scabbard at his hip and gold armour strapped about his chest. The man peers intently into Joshua's rapt face.

'Is Lumaluce in truth your father?'

Joshua nods his head.

'Do you *know* him?' he asks incredulously.

'Nay, not in the physical sense, but I have had communications with him on the astral plain. He is a great hero – a legend among men.'

Joshua gapes in wonder – this man knows his father! A thousand questions spring to his lips, but the man's attention is elsewhere. He's muttering excitedly to himself as again he flicks through the pages of the book. Even though the odd man is deeply absorbed Joshua *has* to ask him a question.

'Sir … *who* are you?'

The man looks up from his book and his intense dark eyes bore into Joshua.

'I am Doctor Dee, the Queen's Conjuror, Mathematician, Astrologer, Alchemist, Scholar and Traveller. In truth it is I who need to know more of you, sir. Lay your left hand upon my shewing stone and let me discover your dark side.'

Joshua does as instructed. Again a pulse of light appears under his fingers and the crystals swirl into a milky grey mist which slowly settles to reveal the dark malevolent image of Leirtod. Joshua springs away from the stone as if it would harm him.

'Leirtod,' says Doctor Dee solemnly.

'You know him, *too*?' gasps Joshua.

'All Alchemists and dabblers in the occult know Leirtod.'

'Occult … ? Do you do *Black Magic*?'

'I study the stars and the movements of the planets. The immensity of their secrets has led me to become impatient with common themes. I seek a greater knowledge of the unknown, which is why I occasionally dabble in witchcraft – as does Leirtod. The dark arts often bring us together.'

Joshua shudders.

'Aren't you scared of him?'

'Why should I be afeared of Leirtod? He seeks your death – not mine.'

'Lucky you!' Joshua mutters under his breath.

Doctor Dee stares thoughtfully into the swirling crystals of the shewing stone.

'You are surely in danger and in sore need of protection,' he adds thoughtfully.

'Leirtod almost got me before ...' Joshua murmurs. 'But my father sent people to help me. They taught me things, gave me *wisdom*,' he adds as he remembers how Athene, Goddess of Wisdom, helped him on his journey in Ancient Greece.

'Then you should arm yourself with wisdom and knowledge once more!' the doctor cries. 'Your ignorance leaves you vulnerable to the Evil One.'

Joshua grasps his words like a lifeline.

'YOU can teach me!' he announces.

'*I*?'

Joshua vigorously nods his head.

'You just said you were a Conjuror, a Mathematician, an Astrologer, an Alchemist, a Scholar and a Traveller. I beg of you, sir ... teach me *EVERYTHING* you know.'

'I am well impressed with your passion, but it would take a lifetime to place into your head all that is in mine,' Doctor Dee replies.

'Let's not waste time,' Joshua answers impatiently. 'Start right away – what's *that*?' he asks as he points to the open page of the big leather-bound book, which depicts an elaborate triangle.

'This is my own personal hieroglyph. Look, it is the symbol for Delta,' he says as he points to the symbol δ. 'It is the Greek letter D. Doctor Dee! Your Greek hieroglyph would be this …' He points to a symbol, χ, in his book. 'This is Chai, it represents a cross.'

Joshua grins.

'*CHAI* … I like the sound of that!'

'Using our own personal hieroglyphics we can communicate in secret, Master Chai, as do all *necromancers*,' the doctor explains.

'What's a necromancer?' Joshua asks warily.

'A person who communicates with the dead,' Dee replies.

Joshua starts in alarm.

'I don't communicate with the dead!'

'Oh, yes you do,' Doctor Dee replies with a knowing smile. 'Lumaluce has been dead for over a thousand years, as has your enemy Leirtod. Yet you communicate with them, do you not?'

Joshua nods.

'Mmm, I suppose so,' he reluctantly agrees.

'Good,' says Doctor Dee. 'It is important to erase superstition and work with a clear mind. A scientist *questions* the unknown rather than standing in fear of it.'

As he speaks, the Doctor turns back to his book and points to an illustration of four zodiac symbols.

'What are these?'

Joshua stares at them and promptly replies, 'Earth, fire, water and air.'

Doctor Dee looks surprised.

'You recognise them!' he exclaims.

Joshua nods.

'Most people who read their horoscopes in the daily papers know which element their star sign is under.'

'We astrologers call the elements the *Trigons*.' The doctor points to another set of symbols. 'Do you recognise these zodiac signs?' he asks.

Joshua shakes his head.

'They are Saturn and Jupiter. Every two hundred years they align with one of the signs of the Trigon.' He stops and peers at the boy, '... which are, Master Chai?'

'Fire, water, earth or air.'

Doctor Dee nods and continues.

'This event changes the zodiac combinations, which is very interesting to an astrologer such as I. Over the centuries the Trigons steadily work their way through all the combinations of the zodiac signs until they return to the primary force which is the *Fiery Trigon*. This great cosmic cycle takes place every nine hundred and sixty years, and it always marks the onset of something *momentous*.'

'Like what?' Joshua asks.

'The birth of Moses and the fall of the Roman Empire are two examples,' the doctor replies.

'Wow! They're pretty momentous,' gasps Joshua. He pauses to look into the doctor's dark brooding eyes. 'What does the present Fiery Trigon mark?'

'I believe it marks the end of the Catholic Church in England.'

Joshua's jaw drops and his mouth hangs open.

'You're *right*!' he gasps 'Everything changed after Henry VIII broke away from the Church of Rome and set up the Church in England.'

'And do not forget the *epochal emergence* of the new star in the heavens,' the doctor adds.

'Hold on!' Joshua exclaims. 'What's an epochal emergence?' he says, stumbling over the long words.

'Ah …' The doctor pauses as he searches for an explanation. 'A new star emerged in the heavens, Nova in Cassiopeia. It was seen as the beginning of a new era, a divine signal to the world's astrologers that global order was in flux and violent changes would come about.'

'Is Leirtod anything to do with these violent changes?' Joshua asks nervously.

'Of course! His evil spirit is drawn to all disruptive forces, but fear not, Master Chai,' Doctor Dee adds in a cheery voice, 'Lumaluce has sent you to me for a purpose.'

He throws an arm about the boy's narrow shoulders.

'Come under my protection, seek knowledge, gain wisdom … and enter an old world on the brink of revolution!'

— 3 —
THE QUEEN'S CONJUROR

Doctor Dee hurries into the Great Hall of Hampton Court, which is hung with jewel-bright tapestries and immense oil paintings – mostly of bearded gentlemen in dark gowns draped with furred collars who seem to frown down in disapproval at the richly dressed courtiers huddled in small groups, deep in intense conversations.

'The Queen is holding court today,' Doctor Dee explains. 'She will hear petitions and everyone here will be keen to have her ear.'

'Do you mean that everybody in this hall has a favour to ask of her?' asks Joshua incredulously.

'Forsooth, they have more than *one* to ask,' the good doctor assures him. 'But Her Majesty will hear only a few.' He nods towards the crowd, which is surging towards the raised dais where an ornate chair is in place.

'They jostle for position, little knowing that the Queen has already made her choice of who she will honour with an interview.'

'What will they petition the Queen for?' Joshua asks.

'Favours. More land, lower taxes, pardon for a crime,

the hand of one of her ladies, her patronage on a business venture,' Doctor Dee replies. He nods towards two men talking excitedly to each other.

'Young Humphrey Gilbert and Martin Frobisher yonder will be heard for sure. One has his mind set on opening up the Northwest Passage; the other is convinced that Christopher Columbus' new world is the lost island of Atlantis.'

'Atlantis?' Joshua mutters. 'I thought Christopher Columbus discovered *America* ... ?'

Doctor Dee looks startled.

'America is what the Spanish call this new territory,' he replies.

Joshua's intrigued.

'So the Spanish call it America but the English know it as the New World?' he asks.

'Aye,' says the doctor with a sharp nod of his head. 'I urge Her Majesty to seize this vast territory before the greedy French and Spanish lay claim to it. *Brytanici Imperii*, I advise the Queen.'

Seeing Joshua's puzzled expression, Doctor Dee stops. 'Do you study Latin, Master Chai?'

'No, sir.'

'Then I will translate,' he says. '*Brytanici Imperii* means the British Empire.'

'So *you* came up with the idea of the British Empire so long ago?'

'I flatter myself 'tis so,' says the doctor with a modest

bow. 'I have written a treatise on the subject and presented it to the Queen who is most interested in my vision of creating rich and powerful English colonies far beyond our home shores. I urge her constantly to take possession of whole land masses as Spain and France so often do.'

'I get the impression that you're not that keen on the French and the Spanish,' teases Joshua.

'Master Chai, they are thieving and acquisitive!' the doctor replies indignantly. 'In truth, they would have the lace from a lady's petticoat!'

Doctor Dee stops as an arrogant-looking gentleman dressed entirely in flowing black robes passes them by. He is swathed on either side by richly liveried servants and followed at a respectful distance by an overweight, red-headed man with small suspicious eyes. The crowd cease their chatter and part to make way for the gentleman, who looks upon all present with contempt.

'Is he a prince?' Joshua whispers.

Doctor Dee shakes his head and pulls down the corners of his mouth.

'Nay … though he behaves as one. He is Sir Francis Walsingham, Secretary of State and one of the Queen's Privy Councillors. The thug at his back is Ingram Frizar, who is as watchful of his master as a bitch in whelp is of her brood.

'Why does Walsingham have a bodyguard?' Joshua asks.

'He is the Master Spy, with a network of undercover operators in his pay. He has enemies everywhere – at home and in Europe. Many would delight in seeing him run through with a blade. He spins a wicked web of lies, secrets and deceit, Master Chai. Be sure you do not get caught up in it.'

Walsingham glowers at Doctor Dee who, unlike all others in the hall, does not bow his head in an act of obeisance. When the Secretary of State has passed by, the doctor continues his tirade against him.

'It is Walsingham who urges Her Majesty to reject my *Brytanici Imperii* theory,' he rages. 'He thinks that the new territories are of doubtful financial value – even though precious ores have already been found there.

Doctor Dee stops to shake his head in disbelief.

'The man is a dunderhead – and a proud one at that!' he mutters darkly.

'He's an idiot!' laughs Joshua. 'America's the richest country in the world.'

Dee gazes at him with interest. 'If only you could share your knowledge with the Queen.'

Joshua grins. 'I could tell her things about America that would blow her mind! New York, Miami, Hollywood, LA. Surfing USA!' he adds with a giggle.

The doctor looks puzzled.

'They're places in America,' Joshua explains.

'They're not on my navigational charts …'

'That's probably because they're not yet discovered!' Joshua tells him. 'Remember I was born in 1991?'

The doctor's thoughtful eyes sweep over the boy.

'You intrigue me, Master Chai,' he says. 'We must talk further, in my private library at Mortlake.'

Their conversation is interrupted by Martin Frobisher, who hurries towards the doctor with a commanding smile on his strong ruddy face.

'I knew he'd be after my favours,' Dee murmurs under his breath.

After an exchange of elaborate bows, Frobisher says with a somewhat smug smile, 'When will my charts and navigational maps be ready, good doctor? The Queen and the Earls of Leicester, Warwick and Sussex have agreed to back my venture to find the Northwest Passage in June.'

The doctor casts an inquisitive eye at the eager adventurer.

'I am surprised that you are so soon equipped to sail, Master Frobisher.'

'The Queen's royal coffers are empty and she is impatient for my expedition to begin. She is eager for the gold that we have been told abounds in the new territories,' Frobisher adds.

'Have you ships, sir?' Doctor Dee enquires.

'Aye. I have three ships and crews to fill them,' Frobisher replies with a bit of a swagger. 'The good ship *Michael* and two scouting ships to boot.'

Doctor Dee waves his hand dismissively.

'The *Michael* is diminutive!' he scoffs. 'She would fit inside Drake's *Golden Hind* four times over.'

'She's seaworthy,' Frobisher insists.

'And *scout ships*! They will never withstand the northern ice fields,' Doctor Dee points out. 'I consider your decision to sail so soon rash and foolhardy, Master Frobisher.'

The man, who is unusually tall compared with all around him, bends to whisper into the doctor's ear.

'The Queen urgently wants *gold*. I cannot risk her wrath by delaying further. We must make use of the summer tides and the long hours of daylight that a June departure would give us,' Frobisher tells him.

'I fear you will live to regret this decision,' says Doctor Dee. 'But as you say, it would be wrong indeed to displease the Queen, who is in the grip of gold fever. I have been working on your charts and maps in my library at Mortlake. They are now complete and ready for your collection, sir.'

'I thank you, good doctor,' Frobisher replies, and with another exchange of bows they part.

'Fool! He will set sail ill-prepared and forsooth shall go adrift,' the doctor mutters to himself as he hurries towards a door richly carved with intertwined red and white roses.

Uniformed guards with sharp raised pikes stand on either side of the door but they immediately relax their weapons to allow the doctor entry then quickly raise them against Joshua.

'The Queen requires me to read her horoscope before she begins the business of the day,' the doctor says as he nods towards the carved doors which lead into the Privy Chambers. 'Remain here, Master Chai. If anybody should question your business, tell them you are Doctor Dee's apprentice.'

Left alone, Joshua feels extremely self-conscious in Dido's baggy tracksuit bottoms and old PE socks, but oddly enough nobody seems to notice. The hustling courtiers are so bound up in court politics and who shall have the Queen's ear that they have neither eyes nor time for anybody else. Joshua spots a bench by a stained glass window and hurries towards it. He sits down and tries to arrange his thoughts.

Can he really have slipped time *again*? 'Either that or I'm at a fancy dress ball,' he thinks to himself. Did Lumaluce manage to side-step Leirtod and remove Joshua into the safe hands of Doctor Dee? If so, he's lucky: at least Joshua doesn't have to convince Dee that Leirtod is evil. He seems to understand that already. But the Court Astrologer must be a busy man; how's he ever going to have time to impart his knowledge to Joshua, who needs it in order to stay alive?

'I'll just have to take what I can get,' Joshua mutters to himself as he throws open the latticed window behind him and gazes out onto the sunken garden, where he's only recently eaten his packed lunch with his classmates. Now it is filled with even more courtiers all queuing to get a place inside the Great Hall. From his high vantage point Joshua overhears some of their conversations.

'I pray good Doctor Dee will conjure Her Majesty into a fine humour,' jokes one gentlemen to another.

'It will take more than magic to persuade the Queen to marry the "Little French Frog", as she calls the simpering Duke of Anjou,' his companion replies.

'England needs an heir,' says the first gentleman. 'And we shall not have one whilst we have a Virgin Queen on the throne!'

'I fear the Queen has eyes for nobody but—' the second gentleman doesn't finish his sentence.

Consumed with curiosity, Joshua hangs out of the window and sees that the crowd are parting and bowing to a handsome young man who carries himself like a king.

'Lord Robert Dudley,' somebody mutters underneath the window. 'He has captivated the Queen with his fine legs and proud eyes.'

'She's *besotted* by him!' his companion adds sourly. 'She never ceases to shower him in gifts and honours – now we are to call him Master of the Horse. Tch!' he sneers. 'We are the laughing stock of Europe!'

Joshua quickly turns away from the window and moves towards the centre of the Great Hall as he hears the guards thumping their pikes on the ground. The doors to the Privy Chambers are flung open and several young ladies issue forth obviously with instructions to seek out the courtiers the Queen has graciously favoured with an audience. Joshua stares at their fine clothes and fluttering veils, and then he blinks in disbelief. Beside a small, squat green-eyed girl with an olive complexion steps another: she is tall and pale with red-gold hair held back from her face by an ornate tiara of twisted metal set with turquoise stones. She is richly dressed in an embroidered brocade dress with flowing sleeves and a high, starched white ruff. The tilt of her pretty head and her proud bearing suggest she might be of noble birth, a princess or a young duchess. What stuns Joshua is the girl's similarity to Dido. She is her living image – Dido's throwback in Tudor England. Intrigued, Joshua watches her search the court and then her eyes come to rest on him. Her jaw drops as her cheeks turn crimson.

'Joshua!' she splutters.

It is her! Joshua physically has to restrain himself from throwing his arms about Dido. She winks and quickly walks away from the courtiers. He follows her into a dark corner where they grip each other's hands as if they were lifelines.

'How did you get here?' they both ask simultaneously.

'I got lost in the maze,' she tells him. 'I went round and round, and at the centre I found the Queen eating peaches with her Ladies of the Bedchamber! When they saw me they all screamed because they thought I was a ghost. Can you believe it Joshua, I look exactly like Queen Elizabeth I when she was a young princess. They brought me back here and dressed me in all this lot ...' she gestures to the long skirt, the white ruff and the tightly boned bodice.

'I am now the Queen's youngest Lady of the Bedchamber and she dotes on me! I can hardly be out of Her Majesty's sight for a minute.'

'Well at least you blend in with the background,' says Joshua. 'I look stupid in your tracksuit bottoms!'

'People will take you for a vagabond.'

He smiles as he notes Dido's Elizabethan use of words. She's obviously picking up the vernacular a lot more quickly than he is.

'So – what happened to *you* in the maze?' she asks.

'As soon as we split up, Leirtod found me. I ran like a wild thing. I was running so fast I didn't notice a giant oak tree in my path. I hit it head on and passed out! When I came round I was in a garden with Doctor Dee.'

'I have just met him in the Privy Chamber,' says Dido. 'They call him the Queen's Conjuror.'

'Doctor Dee *knows* Leirtod and Lumaluce!' Joshua tells her excitedly. 'He's seen them in his crystal ball. He says Lumaluce sent me to him and he'll protect me by giving me knowledge.'

'Well somebody has to!' jokes Dido.

'The doctor's going to *teach* me things and show me magic, Di!' Joshua tells her excitedly.

'You are privileged, Joshua,' she replies in earnest. 'The Ladies of the Bedchamber tell me Doctor Dee is the greatest scholar in Europe. The Queen depends on her Conjuror and will not make a decision without him. The Secretary of State—'

Joshua, who's getting confused with all the strange names and stranger titles, interrupts Dido.

'Is that Sir Francis Walsingham?'

Dido nods quickly and continues.

'Walsingham irritates the Queen but she keeps him close. My friend Thomasina, the little Italian dwarf, says it is because the Queen prefers to have Walsingham as her ally rather than her enemy. Thomasina also told me that the Secretary of State is jealous of the Queen's friendship with Doctor Dee.'

'Well I think Dee's pretty cool,' says Joshua loyally. 'He's discovered this amazing cosmic cycle called the *Fiery Trigon*. It happens every thousand years and it always marks the onset of something momentous.'

'Like what?' Dido asks.

'Like the birth of Moses and the fall of the Roman Empire,' Joshua replies. 'And get this,' he adds excitedly. 'When I asked the doctor what the present Fiery Trigon signified, he said it was the end of the Catholic Church in England!'

Dido's blue eyes grow large with fear.

'The Ladies of the Royal Bedchamber tell me it is a time of great turmoil, with Catholics being burned at the stake and priests on the run.'

'We must take care,' Joshua advises. 'Doctor Dee says there are spies *everywhere* at court.'

'What are we going to do?' Dido blurts out. 'How will we keep in touch if we get separated again?'

'Have you got your mobile?' Joshua asks without thinking.

Dido looks at him and groans in despair. 'There aren't any signals in Elizabethan England!'

The soldiers guarding the Queen's Privy Chambers slam their pikes once more and Doctor Dee emerges, clasping his book and shewing stone. He spots Joshua talking to a red-headed maid and hurries over to them.

'So you found your friend who resembles our gracious sovereign, Master Chai?' he enquires.

'She's a Lady of the Bedchamber,' Joshua explains.

'Excellent, excellent. She is in good company with Thomasina, who is a great favourite of mine. A little maid with a mighty mind,' the doctor says admiringly, then quickly adds, 'Master Chai, my work for the moment is done here. I have further charts to draw up for Her Majesty, but this I can only do in my Observatory at Mortlake. Tomorrow I must leave Hampton Court and,' he says softly, 'you will of course accompany me if you are to stay under my protection.'

If Joshua wants to stay alive he has no choice but to fall in with the doctor's plans – whatever they might be.

'Most certainly, sir,' he replies, and hurries after his master, leaving Dido to return to the Queen's Privy Chambers where her services are required immediately.

— 4 —
THOMASINA

Joshua spends the night with the dogs and the servants in the Great Hall, where the huge log fire gradually dies down low. He sleeps on a bed of straw, which the servants scatter dangerously close to the open fire, but as the fine May day gives way to a chill evening Joshua is glad of the heat from the crumbling ashes. What he doesn't appreciate are the dogs that roam the Great Hall chomping and cracking on bones and leftovers. Tossing and turning, he tries to covers his ears to the sound of their snapping and snarling as they fight over the tastiest morsels. He's rudely awakened at dawn by the arrival of maids who bustle in to sweep away the straw and rekindle the fire. Joshua yawns and rubs his tired eyes.

'What time is it?' he mumbles drowsily.

'Are you blind?' laughs one of the maids.

Joshua wonders if he's missed something obvious, like a big grandfather clock, then he remembers what century he's in. The Tudors don't have clocks – well, not ones on their wrists, anyway!

'It's sunrise,' says the maid as she points to the east window through which he can see the sun rising like a red blood orange.

Joshua is aware of her eyes on his clothes, which are not only bizarre but now covered in straw and dog hairs.

'You cannot sleep in the Great Hall again,' she tells him sharply. 'Tramps and vagrants sleep outside the royal palace.'

Feeling like lowlife, Joshua hurries out into the garden, which is riotous with birdsong. As he dithers about trying to decide where to go to find Dido, a child hurries towards him. She curtsies demurely before him and Joshua realises with a shock that the child is in fact a young woman with the body of a dwarf. She has a gentle smile, dazzling green eyes and raven black hair that is looped and coiled on top of her head.

'I am Thomasina di Signoria. The Lady Dorothea requests your presence in the bowery,' she says.

Joshua's confused. Who's Lady Dorothea and what's a *bowery*?

Seeing his uncertainty, Thomasina adds, 'Your friend awaits you, sir.'

He obediently follows Thomasina to a pretty rose bower where he finds Dido embroidering a silk handkerchief.

'Since when were you *Dorothea*?' he asks with a grin on his face.

'Nobody could understand my name so the Queen gave me a new name … I quite like it,' says Dido with a broad smile. She nods towards Thomasina, who sits down beside her and takes up her embroidery.

'Thomasina's from Italy,' Dido explains. 'We're the

youngest of the Ladies of the Royal Bedchamber – she's teaching me how to embroider.'

'Sit down, Joshua,' Thomasina tells him.

'You're not going to teach *me* how to embroider, are you?' he teases.

'Nay, sir,' the dwarf maid replies. 'We wish only to avoid the prying eyes of Walsingham's spies.'

Joshua immediately sits in the shade of a rose tree that drenches him in its heady perfume.

'Doctor Dee tells me you will travel with him to Mortlake this morning,' says Thomasina in a voice that he now hears has the slightest Italian accent.

Joshua nods unenthusiastically.

'I wish I could stay here at Hampton Court with Di … er, Dorothea!'

'You two are betrothed?' Thomasina enquires.

Dido bursts out laughing.

'I'm too young to be betrothed to anybody.'

'You are twelve years old, the right age for marriage,' Thomasina replies.

Joshua's intrigued.

'Are *you* betrothed, Thomasina?' he asks.

The Italian girl shrugs eloquently.

'No. I am a dwarf. It would be difficult to find somebody to marry me.'

Joshua shuffles uncomfortably. He never meant to ask an insensitive question but Thomasina's not in the least bit embarrassed.

'Anyway,' she adds playfully, 'a husband would interfere with my studies.'

'She reads and writes in FIVE different languages,' says Dido enviously.

'Six,' Thomasina corrects her. 'English, Spanish, Latin, Greek, French – and Italian, which is my mother tongue.'

Joshua grins.

'Wow! Somebody brainier than you, Dido!' he teases. 'Er …' he falters as he tries to remember Dido's Elizabethan name. 'Dorothea is the cleverest girl in our school,' he tells Thomasina.

'You never told me you went to school, Dorothea,' chides the little maid.

Dido throws Joshua an angry look. It's clear that she's been keeping certain things secret and now he's dropped her right in it!

'I *did* go to school,' she tells Thomasina firmly. 'But I don't go now.'

'Doctor Dee's house is like a school,' Thomasina says enthusiastically. 'He has a Laboratory where he practises his alchemy and chemistry, an Observatory where he measures the progress of the stars and a library which houses over three thousand books.'

Joshua is surprised.

'That's a lot of books considering the printing press hasn't long been invented,' he murmurs.

'I myself was with him in Padua when he bought volumes on Plutarch, Euclid and Apollonius. He has books at

Mortlake written by Copernicus and Ptolemy,' Thomasina adds in a voice that's full of awe.

With his newfound enthusiasm for knowledge, Joshua says, 'I'll be eager to study them with the doctor.' Then he adds, 'Pity D-D-Dorothea can't come with us to Mortlake – she loves reading.'

'I can't read Latin and Greek like Thomasina,' Dido points out.

'The doctor has books on every subject,' Thomasina tells them. 'Magic, mathematics, demonology, logic, veterinary science, Islam, logic, zoology, the weather – he's the cleverest man in Europe!' she announces in a voice that's full of admiration.

'How come you know Doctor Dee so well?' Joshua asks.

'He was my father's greatest friend. After Doctor Dee left St John's College in Cambridge he travelled to northern Italy where he and my father studied together at the University of Padua. It is a beautiful city full of learned scholars – and only ten miles from Venice and the vast library of San Marco.'

'Heck! Did they have universities that long ago?' Joshua asks.

'Aye, sir. Oxford University is even older than the one at Padua where my father taught astrology. He built an immense quadrant with which he could measure longitude by the stars. He taught me how the quadrant worked and I helped him with his mathematical calculations.'

'Your father sounds an amazing man,' says Joshua.

'My father was *wonderful*,' Thomasina replies with tears in her green eyes. 'Because I was born inadequate, he knew I would not find a husband. He was not a rich man and therefore could not leave me a vast dowry so he gave me all his knowledge. He taught me everything he knew and took me wherever he went. Some scientists disapproved of a female in their laboratories but they never felt threatened by me, probably because of my mean stature. My father treated me as an equal and drew me into all his discussions. He knew that when he was gone, knowledge would be all I would have to survive on. It was the greatest gift he could have given me – the richest and best dowry that I could possess. He died of the plague when I was fourteen. My mother died in my infancy. I would have been abandoned had it not been for the good Doctor Dee who, on hearing of my father's death, invited me to Mortlake. He needed my assistance in building his own quadrant to measure the stars. It is he who established me at court as a Lady of the Royal Bedchamber,' she ends gratefully.

'Thomasina and the Queen read Greek and Latin together and discuss foreign affairs in French and Italian,' Dido tells Joshua.

'Is there no end to your talents?' he teases.

Thomasina blushes modestly, but Dido is unstoppable in her praise of the Italian girl.

'And she's teaching the Queen how to dance the Volta.'

'What's that?' he asks.

'It's a fashionable Italian dance which has high jumping steps – a bit like ballet,' Dido explains. 'The Queen likes to practise with her favourite, Lord Robert Dudley,' Dido finishes with a wink.

'I keep hearing his name about the court – who is he?' Joshua asks.

'He is the Queen's *favourite*,' Thomasina tells him.

'So why doesn't she marry him?' Joshua asks. 'England needs an heir,' he says, repeating the courtier's words from the day before.

'The Queen's Privy Council urge her to make a wiser and more prosperous match than Robert Dudley who has only fine eyes and finer legs to recommend him,' Thomasina replies. 'Walsingham would have Elizabeth marry Philip of Spain or the Duke of Anjou, but she is not drawn to them, which angers her advisors.'

'What's the point of marrying if you're not in love?' asks Joshua.

'Ssshhh! Guard your tongue, Master Cross!' Thomasina whispers as a dark shadow falls across the sunny bower.

Dido jumps at the sight of the red-headed spy Ingram Frizar, who scowls at Joshua.

'Why doth this tramp tarry so near the Queen's Privy Chambers?' he snaps.

'The good Lady Dorothea is teaching him some simple words so that he may read the Bible, sir,' says little Thomasina with a modest smile.

Frizar ignores her smile and glares at Joshua.

'Who are you?' he barks.

Joshua suddenly remembers Doctor Dee's words.

'I am Doctor Dee's apprentice,' he says in a faltering voice.

'The Queen's *Conjuror*!' sneers Ingram Frizar. 'The fool who fills the Queen's head with necromantic twaddle. He should stick to his star gazing and leave the Queen to the duties of the state!'

Frizar is unaware that Doctor Dee has crossed the lawn and is standing directly behind him.

'You are angry with the Queen's obedient servant?' Dee enquires of Frizar with mock civility.

'You do not fool me with your magic potions and crystal ball!' the spy replies angrily.

'Strange you mock the very things the Queen most admires,' the doctor replies in an amused voice. 'We have just now been talking of dates for her meeting with the Prince of Anjou.'

'It is not for you to advise the Queen on marital matters, conjuror!' sneers Frizar.

'Who the Queen marries is her own affair,' Dee answers coldly. 'Your master, Sir Francis Walsingham, would guide her into the arms of Philip of Spain, but Her Majesty presently leans towards the Duke of Anjou.' Dee gives an eloquent shrug. 'I merely predict auspicious days in her calendar. Midsummer day augurs well … a fine day for romance.'

'*Magician!*' snarls Frizar and seething with fury he stalks out of the bower, which slowly fills up with birdsong and the sweetness of the May morning now that he is gone.

'No doubt he'll repeat every word to the Master Spy,' says Doctor Dee knowingly, 'who will then hurry to the Queen and inform her of all things evil concerning my person.'

'The Queen listens not to *every* word that falls from Walsingham's mouth,' Thomasina says knowingly.

'Aye, maid,' he replies. 'But if she were only to listen to a *half* of what Walsingham spoke of me I would be in mortal danger.'

'Then be vigilant, good doctor. My father always used to say you were the wisest man in Europe – after himself, of course!' she adds with a giggle.

'I wish your father were here to advise me now, little maid,' says the doctor wistfully. 'There is so much to unfold: the new star Nova in Cassiopeia and the emergence of the Fiery Trigon after nearly a thousand years of journeying,' he says in a voice brimming with excitement.

Catching the doctor's mood, Thomasina exclaims, 'Oh, sir! I wish that it were I who was travelling to Mortlake with you. I would love to stand once more in your Observatory and gaze at the stars in the night sky.'

'Then you must makes excuses to your mistress and visit me soon. I have devised new lenses to give me clearer images of the stars and planets.'

'I will visit as soon as I am allowed,' promises Thomasina. Doctor Dee pats her fondly on the head.

'There is no maid in England cleverer than you,' he says admiringly. 'Come walk with me a while.'

When Thomasina and Doctor Dee have left the bower, Joshua and Dido huddle up close and have a whispered conversation.

'Don't leave me, Joshua,' she implores.

'I have to go – I can't stay here. Especially now that Ingram Frizar's told me to get lost! Anyway,' he adds with forced cheeriness, 'Doctor Dee told me Mortlake's only in Wimbledon, which isn't very far from here.'

'But I only know how to get to Wimbledon on the London Underground!' she points out to him.

'You can always grab a donkey!' Joshua says as a joke, but she doesn't laugh.

'The doctor's waving to you, Joshua,' she says as she stands and drops her embroidery at her feet. 'You'd better go,' she adds in a trembling voice.

As Joshua turns to leave, Dido grabs his sleeve.

'Promise me you won't leave me here in Tudor England for ever!'

'I'll come back to you somehow … I promise,' Joshua solemnly replies, but as he walks away from Dido he wonders if they will *ever* meet again …

~ 5 ~
MORTLAKE

When Doctor Dee told Joshua that his house was in the manor of Wimbledon, Joshua assumed, even from a sixteenth-century perspective on travel, that they'd be there in a few hours. The wooden cart they travel in is very uncomfortable, especially when they're bouncing over half-made roads which are rutted and pitted with potholes. And travelling cheek by jowl with passengers who stink so badly nearly causes Joshua to pass out from the stifling stench of their rank body odour. He concentrates on the view: the high verges on the side of the road which are thick with the white of gypsy lace and big-faced white daisies. Behind the hedges in the thick lush pastures are fat cows with their young calves, all with their heads down, munching, watched by the cowherd, a small boy who must be half the age of Joshua.

It's a blessed relief when the cart lumbers to a halt at a tavern where Joshua leaps out, eager to breathe in good clean air. He's also starving! Hunger brings on visions of twenty-first-century culinary delights: burger in a bun with salsa sauce and fries, ice-cold Coke or maybe an extra-thick vanilla shake. When the serving wench plonks down black bread, blood-red beef and a jug of ale, Joshua's heart sinks.

'Eat up,' says the doctor as he bites into his beef. 'We've a long journey ahead of us.'

'It's only *Wimbledon*!' thinks Joshua as he nibbles the bread that's as hard as a rock. 'Ten minutes on the tube, for crying out loud!'

The journey continues. They pass through villages with cottage gardens swarming with a confusion of herbs, vegetables, bluebells and cowslips. Cockerels crow from dung heaps and every household seems to have a pig happily rooting in its pen. Around the villages, the common land is farmed in strips, with carrots and onions drawn up in tidy rows with not an inch of fertile land wasted.

They have been going no longer than three-quarters of an hour when suddenly one of the wagon wheels gets embedded in mud and all the passengers pile out to help the cursing driver to lift it free. With his hands, legs and feet covered in slimy mud, Joshua clambers back into the wagon and wonders if things could get any worse. They do. Half an hour later they lurch to another halt when they come across the body of a dead man on the roadside!

'A vagrant,' says Dee dismissively.

'But he's dead!' gasps Joshua, who's never seen a corpse before.

'Perchance he starved to death,' says Dee.

'What will we do with him?' asks Joshua.

'Roll him into the ditch and abandon him to the wolves,' the doctor replies.

'*Wolves?*' squeaks Joshua nervously. 'Wolves don't live in England. They live in far-off places like Siberia.'

'The wild forests are teeming with wolves,' the doctor assures him.

Wild forests and wolves! Joshua thinks. And this is only Wimbledon. There must be bears and sabre-toothed tigers in Watford!

The body's removed or, more accurately, chucked into the ditch, and they continue their journey, which is further interrupted by the startling appearance of two wild boars. They're *enormous*, with long horns, curly tails and little piggy eyes full of anger. The two hairy males charge at each other and lock horns, then grunt viciously as they twist each other's heads as if they would happily rip them off!

'Gettout of it!' bawls the driver as he cracks his whip against the boars' ample bottoms. Squealing angrily, the wild boars kick up their back legs and gallop away into the dense oak forest.

The eventful journey ends when the driver pulls the lumbering cart horses to a halt and calls out, 'Mortlake.'

It is wonderful to step down and watch the swaying cart, which is no more than a tub on wheels, rattle down the track to Cheam, where Joshua imagines black bears and panthers might roam.

In the pale twilight Joshua hurries after the doctor, who

guides him through narrow lanes hardly wide enough for both of them to walk side by side.

'It reminds me of Devon,' chuckles Joshua as he and the doctor keep bumping into each other.

'Hah! You have travelled so far, Master Chai,' exclaims the doctor.

'Devon's not far. Only about four hours on the motor-way—'

Joshua stops. A journey to Devon in Elizabethan England would be the equivalent of Joshua crossing the Alps on a bicycle. So he rephrases his sentence and says, 'It is a long journey but well worth the effort.' Joshua smiles to himself as he realises that he, like Dido, is slipping into the Elizabethan vernacular.

The steep hedgerows that flank their path are sweet with the pungent perfume of wild flowers. Joshua sniffs deeply.

'What's that smell?' he asks.

'Wild violet and musk rose,' the doctor replies.

'I've never smelt anything so lovely.'

'Perchance you hail from a barren land if you are not familiar with the smell of wild violet. It is as common as the daisy,' the doctor stares at the boy with interest. 'Where *do* you hail from, Master Chai?'

Joshua racks his brains trying to think where the London Eye would have been in the days of Elizabeth I.

'Southwark,' he replies. 'Round the corner from the Globe Theatre.'

Doctor Dee looks shocked.

'You inhabit a dangerous part of the city. It houses London's scoundrels and stinks like a sewer. Have you met Will Shakespeare and the Queen's Men at the Globe?'

'Well, not *personally* – though I have seen his plays.'

'I like not the south bank of the Thames,' says Doctor Dee disapprovingly.

'My mum likes it,' Joshua replies staunchly.

'Does she keep a brothel?'

Enraged, Joshua stops dead in his tracks.

'My mum is a respectable widow woman!'

'How does she survive?'

'She cooks.'

Doctor Dee laughs scornfully.

'The wife of the legendary Lumaluce *cooks*!'

'My dad left this world in too much of a hurry to sort out his finances,' Joshua tells him sharply. 'My mother supports me and my brother by cooking fish and chips, which she's very good at, actually,' he adds a trifle huffily.

Dee stops and looks at him.

'Ah, you never mentioned you had a brother, Chai. Is he not, like you, threatened by the evil forces of Leirtod?'

Joshua shakes his head.

'Lumaluce told me that though my brother was his natural son he is not his spiritual heir … if you know what that means?' he adds self-consciously.

'Indeed,' the doctor replies briskly. 'I am deeply involved in the spirit world. It exists alongside the reality of our daily life, yet most mortals neither question nor challenge what is around them. They take for granted the air that we breathe, the ground that we stand on, the stars over our heads. The population can be likened to a herd of cattle continuously filling their bellies: they neither question it nor argue a good case against it. Most are content in the age-old belief that the Earth is the centre of the universe with the Moon circling it.' He breaks off to laugh mockingly. 'The stars are no more than gaudy baubles which flit like the angels flit around the heavenly sphere!'

'What! So you haven't discovered the Solar System yet?' Joshua asks.

'Prithee, sir, do not interrupt me,' says Doctor Dee impatiently. 'We scholars and scientists can no longer ignore the knowledge that is at our fingertips. Maps are being drawn up that chart the seas. New worlds that we never dreamed of are being discovered. Crystals and mirrors give us clear views of the heavens, which are teeming with stars and planets. It is a brave new world that we enter, Master Chai. Aye, even though we risk our lives pushing at the edges of the known universe in the pursuit of knowledge.'

'What's wrong with a bit of self-education?' Joshua asks.

'In these times science is a dangerous subject. Sir Francis Walsingham considers it a form of devil worship, punishable with death. If he knew what mysteries I unfold here in my Laboratory at Mortlake he would torch the building and burn my family and me at the stake for high treason.'

Their conversation comes to an end as they turn a corner and a large house flanked on either side by old elm trees looms into view. To the right of the house Joshua can see a pretty little Gothic church, which he assumes is the doctor's own private chapel, and beyond that nothing but dense woodlands, probably teeming with wolves, thinks Joshua with a shudder.

'Be assured, Master Chai. We will talk further about Lumaluce, but behind closed doors with no fear of eaves-droppers or spies,' says Doctor Dee as he strides up the path and bangs on the carved front door. 'And we will track down the evil one who pursues you – on that I give you my troth!'

The door is flung open by a woman half the age of the doctor.

'Husband!' she cries. 'How was your journey?'

'Comfortable, Mistress Jane,' he replies.

Joshua bites his tongue and remains politely silent. COMFORTABLE!! He's been more comfortable on a roller-coaster ride at Blackpool Pleasure Beach.

'Behold my new apprentice,' says Dee as Joshua bows formally before the lady of the house. 'Master Chai was gravely agitated by the presence of wolves on our journey,' Dee adds with a mischievous grin.

Mistress Jane smiles warmly at Joshua.

'Welcome to Mortlake, Master Chai. Come. I have a fine supper prepared for you.'

Feeling grubby and a bit windy after his raw meat lunch, Joshua blushes as he asks, 'Er, is there somewhere I could wash my hands and … ?'

'I will show you to the garderobe.'

Mistress Dee doesn't need to tell him where the toilet is. As she guides him down a long oak-panelled corridor, Joshua can smell it about twenty feet away! The pong is vile. And he's got to go in there and add to it. But at least it's not a hole in the ground, which was all he used at Hampton Court. This one has a seat over a hole in the ground. As he hunts around for something resembling toilet paper – a dock leaf would do – Joshua vows he will never *ever* complain about the school toilets. At least they've got a flush system!

Supper is much better than lunch. A young chicken cooked in wine and honey, warm bread, oysters, a curd cheese and a bowl of red cherries, which are the sweetest fruit that Joshua has ever bitten into. The doctor drinks sweet mead but Joshua sticks to water drawn from the well in the garden. After the delicious meal Joshua feels full and sleepy, but the doctor, greatly refreshed by the food, is keen to show him the library.

'Come, Master Chai – you have much to learn if you are to catch up with me!' he teases as they make their way down labyrinthine corridors lit only by a sputtering candle which Dee carries in his hand.

When Joshua feels like he's walked half a mile from the main body of the house, Dee leads him into a dark room, which echoes with their footsteps. The doctor lights candles in sconces and the room blazes into light. Joshua gasps in disbelief. It is the size of a small church and it's stacked from floor to ceiling with books.

'My library,' says Dee with a ring of pride in his voice. 'The finest in Europe. There are more than three thousand books here and I have read them all. When I studied mathematics at Cambridge, my taste for knowledge was thwarted by a distinct lack of books. A mere four and fifty books the university library housed. I determined to have my own library so I set about collecting books on my travels in Europe.'

'Thomasina told me you bought books in Padua,' says Joshua as his eyes rake up and down the shelves.

'Ah, sweet Thomasina. If it were not for her tiny stature I would have taken her as my wife. Instead I married one of Elizabeth's favourite handmaidens, Jane. She has a comely face and brought a modest dowry. But as for brains, she is as empty-headed as a sieve. Thomasina has the brains of ten men and she is as sharp as she is wise. I worked with her father in Padua. Ah, those were happy days when I could study at my leisure …' says Dee with a heavy sigh. 'Now I am Court Astrologer, the Queen demands my whole attention. She hardly dares visit the garderobe unless I tell her the planets bode well! If I don't attend court as oft as she likes, then she comes hither to

Mortlake to consult with me. As you know, Master Chai, Sir Francis Walsingham has no fondness for me or my studies. He would have me publicly disembowelled if he could find me guilty of something treasonable … one day he might do so, but *not* while I enjoy the Queen's protection.'

'Why does he hate you so much?' Joshua enquires.

'Jealousy, insecurity,' the doctor replies with a shrug. 'He thinks I mix potions and stick pins in wax images! What a fool. Let me tell you a secret, Master Chai,' the doctor adds with a chuckle. 'When the English navy beat the Spanish Armada, word went round the court that I had put a spell on the Spanish. Oh, I laughed so much at the prospect tears flowed down my face and drenched my beard!'

Joshua, who believes the doctor capable of anything, asks, 'Did you?'

'Nay. In truth I merely used my knowledge.' He picks up a book from the long oak table that runs almost the length of the library which, at that moment, is golden in the soft glow of candlelight.

'This is one of the many books I possess concerning the subject of weather patterns and meteorology. I have metal instruments in my Laboratory that contract or expand according to the weather system. On this occasion, when the Armada was forming in the Atlantic waiting to meet up with Sir Francis Drake's fleet, my instruments indicated that an immense electrical storm was brewing just off the coast of Plymouth Sound. When the Queen urged me to consult with my almanac, I pretended to do so, when all the time I was immersed in my meteorological observations. When she finally demanded an answer from me, should the fleet sail out and meet up with the Spanish, yeah or nay? I said nay, the day did not augur well. I did not go into technical detail, but she took me at my word and withheld her navy from sallying forth. Later that day the storm hit the Atlantic like the angry hand of God! It blew the Spanish ships up to Scotland and over to Ireland where most of them sank.'

Bells are ringing in Joshua's head.

'We read about this at school last week!' he exclaims. 'The Armada were smashed to smithereens – it was a complete victory for England.'

'Aye, we routed the Spanish right well and good,' says the doctor with undisguised relish. 'But it was not a spell that saved Her Majesty's navy – it was scientific knowledge!'

'She really thinks it was all down to your genius?' Joshua asks.

Doctor Dee nods and answers, 'The Queen trusts me and has a great affection for my Almanac. It was I who chose the most auspicious day in the calendar for her coronation, a day that augured well for the Queen and her people. The 15th of January 1559. A tempestuous blustery day when the streets of London were lined with cloth of gold and Her Majesty rode through wind and rain like a radiant goddess. The populace adored her, and they still do, Master Chai. She is a good and fair monarch is our good Queen Bess,' he adds fondly.

'Does the Queen know how much Walsingham hates you?' Joshua asks.

Doctor Dee nods.

'I suspect she does but she never refers to it. Her Majesty is a cunning stateswoman. Whilst she watched her father take many wives and behead two of them, including her own mother, the young Princess Elizabeth learnt great patience. Even when disclaimed as illegitimate with no right to the throne she remained quiet and withdrew into the background. If she had put forward an opinion and been strident and protesting in her manner, she would have been dead long ago, betrayed by her sister Mary and indeed by her father, whose greatest love was ever for himself. She learnt much about political manipulation in those terrible years in the shadows and she uses those very skills with her Privy Council now that she is Queen. Her trick is to play one off against the other ... let them do mischief which she is able to disassociate herself from. If all falls out well she will take the credit; if it should be otherwise she will lay no claim to it and let her council take the brunt.'

Dee smiles mischievously. 'Shall I tell you how I know that the Queen distrusts Walsingham?'

Joshua nods eagerly.

'Her Majesty is well aware that Walsingham tampers with her letters. When I am sent abroad on a mission of the realm the Queen and I use a secret code number.' He drops his voice to a whisper as if there were spies concealed in the panelwork of the library. 'It is the alchemist's lucky number, 007, and it signifies that the letter is from me to her and nobody else: *it is for her eyes only.*'

Joshua jumps in surprise.

'You nicked that from a James Bond film!'

The doctor shakes his head in confusion.

'James Bond ... is he a spy?'

Joshua grins.

'Aye, sir – *the best!*'

In the spluttering candlelight, with owls hooting in the garden, Doctor Dee shows Joshua some of his most precious books.

'Regard my treasures, Master Chai,' says Doctor Dee as he reverently picks up one faded volume after another. 'Commentaries on Greek geometrics, a Treatise on Magic written in Hebrew, an ancient cabala, a Book of Experiments more than a thousand years old and an ancient Ordinal of Alchemy penned in the mists of time.'

Joshua smothers a huge yawn. He *must* stay awake so that he can learn from the doctor, but he can barely keep his eyes open. Seeing the boy's weary expression, Dee concedes that it is late.

'I have much to teach you, Master Chai. Tomorrow I will show you my Laboratory and Observatory.'

Doctor Dee guides Joshua through the labyrinthine corridors, back into the house, which is cold and pitch black. Joshua's room overlooks the garden now steeped in moonlight.

'Sleep well, apprentice,' says Dee as he closes the door and leaves Joshua with a single spluttering candle.

Joshua smiles.

'Goodnight, master.'

His bed is made of coarse cloth stuffed with straw and rosemary to make it smell sweet. Joshua pulls the thin cover over his shivering body. Right now he'd sell his back teeth for his warm feather duvet at home in Shakespeare's Chippy, Isabella Street, Southwark ... on the banks of the swiftly flowing River Thames.

6

GARDEROBES AND DISTILLATIONS

The next morning, the house is stirring when the sun is hardly up in the sky. What is it with these Elizabethans and rising early, Joshua wonders as he sticks his fingers in his ears in an attempt to block out the sound of clattering feet and barking dogs. Bits of straw and spikes of rosemary poke into his back preventing further sleep, so he gets up and heads for the garderobe, which reeks even worse than the previous day. As Joshua perches nervously on the wooden seat he swears that from now on he's going to go into the open fields and relieve himself, or remain constipated throughout his mysterious sojourn in Elizabethan England!

Mistress Dee serves Joshua warm bread and honey from a honeycomb for breakfast, along with a tankard of ale, which Joshua declines.

'My good husband bids you join him after you have broken your fast,' says Mistress Dee.

Joshua hasn't a clue what she means.

'Is that something I do in church?' he asks uncertainly.

Mistress Dee smiles at him.

'Nay. It is the first meal of the day, Master Chai,' she explains.

Joshua grins.

'Ah, break … fast! Gottit!'

But finding Doctor Dee's not easy. The corridors interconnect with rooms and hallways which dip down into cellars or lead up to high landings overhung with precarious balconies. Lost and confused, Joshua rambles around until he hears a crashing sound below stairs. He hurries down the cellar steps, which lead into a cavernous room dominated by what he assumes is a huge wooden pulpit. There he finds Doctor Dee muttering to himself as he pores over a book propped up on the pulpit.

'Laggard, Master Chai!' exclaims the doctor when Joshua hurries in.

'Laggard … ?' Joshua puzzles over the word.

'You rise late of a morning,' says Dee reproachfully.

You mean I don't get up with the dawn chorus, Joshua thinks to himself, but his response is polite enough.

'I was tired, sir.'

'Fatigue is an unnecessary waste of time,' the doctor replies briskly. 'Come hither and join me at my Alchemist's desk.'

Joshua approaches the huge desk, which is surrounded by six stills bubbling over steaming cauldrons of water.

'I'm distilling potions,' the doctor explains. 'Each of the stills contains a different combination of eggshells and horse dung.'

'Nice!' Joshua mutters under his breath.

'The right combination will produce a palliative for headaches, haemorrhage and heartburn. The ill-balanced mixtures once imbibed will produce symptoms of gas and wind.'

With the garderobe always at the forefront of his mind, Joshua nervously asks, 'You're not going to ask *me* to imbibe, are you, sir?'

'That would be discourteous,' Dee assures him. 'I have dames in the village who sample my potions for a penny then relate to me the details of their condition. It is most alarming to hear of their complaints and yet they return for more samples – and indeed more pennies,' he adds with a chuckle.

Joshua knows for sure that he wouldn't go anywhere near the horse dung and eggshell mixture even if the doctor were to offer him a *thousand* pennies!

'Some of my more successful remedies I have preserved,' says Dee as he gestures towards his many shelves lined with bottles of different hues.

'I have mixtures of spearmint syrup, red fennel, liverwort, dates, mace, celery, turnip and camomile – but this,' says the doctor as he lifts a bottle from the shelf and places it with reverential care on his Alchemist's desk, 'I have *not* distilled.'

Joshua gazes at the bottle of earthy red powder.

'It looks like cayenne pepper!'

'Pepper! Forsooth, Master Chai!' cries Dee. 'It is my most precious tincture, one which is much sought after by alchemists,' he adds mysteriously.

Joshua peers again at the earthy red powder but he's *still* not impressed. He doesn't want to upset the doctor, so he keeps his mouth shut.

'If you were to gaze at it for the waxing and waning of three moons you would not guess its elemental powers,' the doctor says as he picks up the bottle and swirls the contents.

Joshua notices that the normally wise face of the doctor is suddenly possessed by a wild, obsessive look. 'This is powder from the Philosopher's Stone. It turns base metal into *gold*!' whispers Doctor Dee. 'A single ounce is capable of producing 22,000 pounds of gold!'

'WOW! That's amazing,' exclaims Joshua who's finally impressed. 'Have you tried it out yet?'

Dee shakes his head.

'I cannot tamper with the Philosopher's Stone,' the doctor replies in a shocked voice. 'If I am to explore alchemy at a level as deep and sacred as this, I need spiritual guidance.'

'A priest?' Joshua enquires.

'There are no priests in England, Master Chai. Well not unless you count those in hiding, of which there are many,' Dee replies as he returns the precious bottle to the shelf.

'Who can help you, then?' Joshua asks.

'You will meet him soon. He is presently helping Sir Walter Raleigh but soon he will visit *me*,' Dee says with barely suppressed excitement. 'Meanwhile I have much to impart to you, Master Chai. Come, I will show you my Observatory.'

As Joshua follows the doctor up a long winding flight of stairs, he wonders how Dee manages to divide his time between the demands of the Queen, his three thousand books, his bubbling stills, his stargazing, his meteorological interests and his mathematical charts.

They climb up and up until they come to the very top of the house, where the doctor ushers Joshua into his private Observatory, which is built of timber and glass. Because of its airy structure Joshua feels as if the room is suspended in space, like an eagle's eyrie hung high over a forest. It is full of globes, maps, birth charts, almanacs, compasses, crystals, lenses, mirrors and a huge metal structure.

'This is the mathematical Quadrant which the little maid Thomasina helped me erect,' Dee explains. 'With this I first located the emerging new star Nova Cassiopeia … but it was not enough. I needed something more precise –

something that would give me a clearer view of distant objects.'

'Like a telescope!' suggests Joshua with a grin.

'*Exactly*! I would not have succeeded without the help of Thomasina. She recorded much of her father's scientific experiments in Padua. He worked closely with a brilliant young student called Galileo and together they assembled lenses and mirrors to gaze at the stars from Galileo's tower. I visited it once myself and was mightily impressed. Thomasina's father is long dead, God rest his soul, but Galileo works on. He will one day succeed, for he hath a brilliant mind and a great vision. I have not his tools nor his instruments, but Thomasina and I constructed a crude device of lenses and mirrors and we were thus able to observe the new star with greater accuracy.'

As Doctor Dee tells his story, his smooth face grows pink with excitement.

'It was the most auspicious astronomical phenomenon since the appearance of the Star of Bethlehem at the birth of Christ ...' The intensity in Dee's voice suddenly falters and his face hardens. 'Sadly, my study of Nova Cassiopeia and how she moved in relation to the fixed stars nearly cost me my life.'

'Did Walsingham get wind of it?' Joshua asks.

The doctor's brow creases.

'Speak clearly, Master Chai!' he barks impatiently.

Joshua quickly rephrases his sentence into the Elizabethan vernacular.

'Walsingham did not approve your findings?'

'He was on a witch hunt – and *I* was the hunted one!' seethes the Doctor. 'Through his network of spies, Walsingham spread the rumour that I was a threat to the universe! The Privy Council, my Lords Hatton, Burghley, Cecil and, of course, Walsingham himself, rejected the new star Nova Cassiopeia outright.'

Doctor Dee mournfully shakes his head.

'When the great Polish mathematician Copernicus announced that the Sun was the centre of the universe, learned scholars across Europe acclaimed his findings – it was a great leap forward for scientists! But Walsingham and the Queen's Privy Council insisted that the Earth *must* remain the centre of the universe. How could a star move beyond the celestial place, which was heaven itself, Walsingham asked me. When I explained the phenomenon that was taking place he promised to put my head on a spike over London Bridge!'

Dee shrugs sadly.

'So much for science. It was fortunate indeed that Nova Cassiopeia suddenly disappeared, never again to be seen. I could no longer chart her movements across the sky, thus I had nothing further to say on the subject and consequently I kept my head.'

Joshua looks towards the doctor's desk scattered with maps and measuring instruments.

'But you *still* practise astrology?' he enquires.

'God's Wounds! Aye, Master Chai,' exclaims the doctor.

'Fools and babes may gaze up at the stars and consider them nothing more than decorations in the heavenly sphere. Not so we men of science. We continue to map the movements of the stars and planets, but I for one keep my findings to myself and drop not a word to the Master Spy. In Germany and Holland, aye, and in Italy and Constantinople, men of knowledge can speak out, but in England we are under threat. The new age is dawning abroad but the morning light has not reached our shores.'

'It *will*. I *know*, sir,' Joshua tells him emphatically.

'You give me hope, young Chai,' the doctor says with a faint smile. 'Now, regarding a privy matter,' he says as he lowers his voice. 'You recall I mentioned a person might visit me ... ?'

Joshua nods.

'Aye. The one who presently resides with Sir Walter Raleigh,' he replies.

'Speak softly, Master Chai,' says the doctor. 'Even walls have ears.'

Joshua casts a nervous glance over his shoulder, then leans forward to catch whatever the doctor has to tell him.

'Know you of Skryers, sir?' Dee whispers.

Joshua shakes his head.

'I've never even heard the word before.'

'A Skryer is a spiritual medium,' Doctor Dee explains. 'Sir Walter Raleigh will send such a man hither. He travels under the name of Edward Kelley, but if Walsingham or any of his Agents Provocateurs were to hear of his coming

I would be arrested and tried for witchcraft. The sentence for which is public disembowelment, usually on a feast day in order to provide the holiday crowd with good entertainment.'

Joshua visibly pales.

'Why do you risk meeting him?' he asks incredulously.

'Because he can give me *knowledge*, Master Chai!' Dee replies with that wild look back in his eye. 'Knowledge is power!' he mutters distractedly while pacing the room. 'I have so much to learn, so much to discover ... and all in a brief lifetime of three score years and ten.'

'But Thomasina told me that you have more knowledge than ΛNYBODY in England!' Joshua exclaims.

'It is not enough, Chai,' the doctor replies. 'I MUST have *more*!'

At Hampton Court, Dido has already met the Skryer Edward Kelley. He arrived in the company of Sir Walter Raleigh who is presently sitting at his ease in the royal Privy Chambers reciting in a voice that has a rich Devon accent his latest love poem dedicated to his paramour: the Queen. Ranged in favoured lines around the Queen are her ladies. First are the four Ladies of the Bedchamber: Lady Dorothea (Dido), Lady Thomasina, Lady Bess Throckmorton and Lady Mary Sydney. Second come the Queen's eight women of the Privy Chamber, older women who keep everything running smoothly, then finally her half-dozen Maids of Honour. These young girls are all daughters of rich and titled families who pay the Queen handsomely for the honour of having their girls at the heart of court life.

As Raleigh beguiles the Queen with his fulsome poem, Dido whispers to Thomasina, 'He's *flirting* with her!'

Thomasina shrugs as if Dido were stating the obvious.

'Raleigh has entertained Her Majesty since the first time they met on a rainy day in London. He threw his rich velvet cape into a muddy puddle so that the Queen might not step into the puddle and dirty her shoes! The Queen was much amused. She laughed at the sight of the cloak seeping into the mud, then she stepped onto it, thus keeping her feet dry. Raleigh's been one of her favourites ever since.'

Thomasina thoughtfully observes the laughing young man beside the Queen.

'He charms her right well and is a pleasant change from her sombre Privy Council,' she remarks.

Dido gazes at the Queen's advisors: Lords Hatton, Burghley, Cecil and Walsingham, all darkly clad and grim of face, ranked behind the Queen like looming black eagles. Witty Raleigh in his bright, elegant clothes must be light relief compared with these granite-faced statesmen!

'Raleigh's a clever man,' Thomasina continues. 'He's a poet, sailor, soldier and an explorer to boot. He discovered the first English Colony in the New World, which he named Virginia in honour of Her Majesty. She was well pleased – though she would have been best pleased if he'd returned with his ship's hull loaded with gold instead of potatoes and tobacco! The Queen says Raleigh has style but no substance and therefore denies him entry into her Privy Council, which he most passionately desires.

'Yet she is entertained by him,' Dido points out.

'She admires a man with a shapely calf and a twinkling eye,' Thomasina answers knowingly.

'He has an eye for all the Queen's ladies,' Dido notes as she catches Raleigh smiling charmingly at pretty Bess Throckmorton. The Queen catches his smile and frowns disapprovingly.

'Dorothea!' she calls out. 'Throw open the casement – Sir Walter has made me warm with his love poem.'

'Yes, Your Majesty,' says Dido as she bobs a curtsey and turns to the latticed window, which she opens and gazes down from onto the rose garden below. She notices a large man striding purposefully up and down the borders between the blooms. He is dressed like a monk in a cloak with a cowled hood. Dido would not have given him a second glance had she not caught sight of shifty Ingram Frizar furtively watching the movements of the man in the rose bower. As Dido is about to turn back into the room, a sudden gust of wind blows the hood from the man's head, revealing that his right ear has been lopped off. Horrified at the sight of the livid red scar left by the severing of the ear, Dido cries out, 'Hahh!'

'What ails you, child?' enquires the Queen when she hears Dido's stifled cry. 'Have you a chill?'

'Nay, Ma'am. I'm perfectly well,' Dido replies as she quickly turns and curtsies to the Queen. 'It was the shock of seeing a man yonder with his right ear lopped clean from his head.'

Dido's description of the man causes Sir Walter Raleigh to move to the open window and peer out.

'Ah, know you this man who hath no ear, Sir Walter?' the Queen asks suspiciously.

Dido notes that Walsingham leans forward, his body tensed with expectancy as he waits for Raleigh's answer to the Queen's question.

'In truth, Ma'am, he is in my employment,' Raleigh answers, and though he smiles merrily, his voice is awkward. He pauses as if carefully choosing his words. 'I brought him down from the county of Lancashire.'

'Lancashire!' the Queen cries as if it were the dark side of the moon.

'Aye, my lady,' Raleigh replies with a little laugh. 'He is a most excellent chartist. I am most anxious to accurately record my sighting of the new colony Virginia. I am a mulehead at such things and therefore took Master Kelley into my employ for this very purpose.'

The Queen is not appeased by his clever explanation.

'Pray tell me why a charter of maps with the lopped ear of a forgerer to boot does loiter in my rose bower?' she asks archly.

'I bid him wait there for me,' Raleigh answers humbly.

'Then bid him hence, sir, or he will lose his other ear!'

the Queen snaps, and rising from her chair she brings the romantic poetry reading to an abrupt end.

As Raleigh hurries from the room, Walsingham crosses to the open window, which he looks out of, clearly eager for a glimpse of Raleigh's guest: the one-eared man from the county of Lancashire.

7

ZOPPO MAGNUS

Having received a hefty fee from Sir Walter Raleigh, Edward Kelley obediently copies his master's navigational maps charting the coastline of Virginia. But copying is merely an artful subterfuge. What Raleigh *really* wants of Kelley is his skrying skills. Sir Walter and several titled gentlemen of the court regularly meet with playwrights and poets at Durham House, Raleigh's opulent riverside mansion, where they indulge in Black Magic and dabble in the occult. Raleigh's 'School of the Night' requires the services of a spiritualist and there is no better Skryer in England than one-eared Edward Kelley. Walsingham's network of spies have alerted their master to the dark events that regularly take place at Durham House, and Ingram Frizar is dispatched with all speed to watch around the clock the comings and goings in Raleigh's mansion.

Catching red-headed Ingram Frizar spying on him for the second night running throws Sir Walter Raleigh into a frenzy of fear. He is well aware that skrying is an imprisonable offence. Much as he enjoys Kelley's company, he knows that he must get rid of him before he is further incriminated. Raleigh hastily pens a letter to his good friend Doctor Dee, who shares his interest in the occult.

'*My good Doctor Dee,*' the note reads ...

You are already privy to the knowledge that under my roof resides the excellent Skryer Edward Kelley. He hath much impressed me with his skrying skills and he hath contributed greatly to my School of the Night parleys, where he showed himself most willing and able to summon up spectres and visions that took our very breath away. Sadly the Secretary of State, Sir Francis Walsingham, has been alerted to Kelley's whereabouts and his loathsome spy, Ingram Frizar, prowls constantly at my gate. I fear for Kelley. He hath already lost one ear – I would not have him lose his head! Therefore, good friend, I send my Skrying agent with Edward Kelley sooner than we planned. Use him well. Keep him safe and hide him if Walsingham should come knocking on your door.

Farewell.

The Skryer's arrival at Mortlake turns the peaceful household into a hotbed of anger and mistrust. His presence transforms Dee from the wise doctor that he is into a doting slave who cannot get enough of Kelley. Joshua's feelings could not be more different. The minute he lays eyes on the Skryer standing boldly in the hall taking in his surroundings, which are not as grand by half as those of Durham House, Joshua's skin creeps. He shivers as he stares at the man in the cowled hood which gives Kelley the appearance of a monk, but a deep scar the length of his right cheek belies a pious nature. The Skryer bows low to the doctor as he introduces himself.

'I have come hither at the recommendation of Sir Walter Raleigh,' he announces. 'I also have the patronage of the Earls of Leicester, Pembroke and Northumberland,' he adds with a ring of pride in his deep voice. 'I am not a conjuror or a caller-up of devils but a master of Archemastry, an experimental observation involving the use of crystal gazing.'

Dee bows humbly before him as if *he* were the pupil and Kelley the master. 'I am most indebted to Sir Walter for sending you to my home, where you are most welcome, sir.'

Dee turns to Joshua who's lurking in the background. 'This is my apprentice, Master Chai.'

Edward Kelley's brow furrows as his penetrating eyes rake up and down the boy's body as if he were searching for something.

'Nay. He is not called Chai ... he bears another name.' The Skryer's eyes scour Joshua's face. 'I see that the boy is overshadowed by the forces of evil.'

Joshua gasps in surprise.

'How do you know that, sir?'

'I do not see *only* with my eyes,' the Skryer replies haughtily, then he turns away from Joshua as if his business with him is over ... at least for the moment.

Doctor Dee ushers his visitor into the parlour, where Mistress Dee waits to greet him. The second she sees Edward Kelley, Mistress Dee gasps and puts a hand to her throat as if she, like Joshua, is overwhelmed by a sense of unease.

'This is my good wife—'

Kelley interrupts the doctor.

'She is Jane, formerly a lady of the court, now mother to your two children, Arthur and Katherine.'

Mistress Dee visibly pales, but Dee beams with pleasure.

'You honour me with your knowledge, sir,' he says as he leads his guest towards the food laid out on the table. 'Pray, refresh yourself.'

Kelley shakes his head so vehemently the cowled hood falls from his head. Joshua and Mistress Dee recoil at the sight of his severed ear but Doctor Dee registers neither shock nor surprise. Kelley coolly replaces the hood and says, 'I take neither flesh nor drink before a spiritual séance. It is important to cleanse the body. I have washed my hands and face, cut my nails and shaved my beard in readiness for our crystal gazing. Now if you will show me the way, good doctor, I am eager to begin.'

Joshua wishes with all his heart that he could stay with Mistress Dee and her babies, but Dee beckons him to follow and he dutifully does so. As he reluctantly mounts the flight of stairs that lead to the Observatory, Joshua wonders why he feels such an aversion to Edward Kelley.

He certainly doesn't like his bold manner, nor does he like his lopped-off ear, but it is something *more* sinister than that … the Skryer reminds him of Leirtod!

They enter the high airy Observatory, where Dee places his shewing stone on his desk. Without waiting for an invitation Kelley seats himself and starts to take deep breaths, all the while staring into the stone. Within minutes Joshua sees that Kelley's dark eyes mirror the swirling milky white crystals. Suddenly the Skryer cries out, '*Uriel*!'

Joshua has no idea who Kelley's talking about. Doctor Dee leans forward in his chair, eager to speak, but Kelley raises his hand and stops him.

'Look into the stone,' he says in a strangely melodious chant that is quite unlike his normal voice.

Joshua and the doctor simultaneously gaze into the stone … where Joshua sees nothing but churning crystals. Not so the doctor, who gasps in surprise.

'What can you see?' Joshua asks him impatiently.

'An angel!' Dee replies in a rapt voice.

'It is the Angel Uriel, who buried Adam's body in the cold earth,' Kelley announces. 'Uriel who revealed to the prophet Enoch the heavenly luminaries.'

Dee sits bolt upright in his chair.

'May I ask the angel a question?' he says to Kelley, who is in such a deep trance-like state his face and eyes have turned blank and lifeless.

Kelley doesn't reply. He waits as if for instructions then nods abruptly.

'You may speak.'

'Did the prophet Enoch record the language of God – the language that Adam used to name the birds and the beasts?' Doctor Dee asks.

'This book was revealed to Adam in Paradise,' says Kelley melodically. 'The words written there have come straight from the mouth of God, uncorrupted by the fall of man.'

Doctor Dee leans towards the shewing stone and Joshua sees his body quiver with excitement.

'Hahhh!' he exclaims in a rapture of delight. 'I see Adam's Book!'

Joshua peers into the stone once more – why can't *HE* see these things too?

'How may I read it?' the doctor asks Kelley. 'Where may I find it?'

'Only Michael the Archangel can light your way,' Kelley murmurs and then a shudder goes through him, like a shock of electricity. 'Ah …' he sighs as he slumps exhausted onto the desk.

Doctor Dee turns to Joshua, who is shocked to see his master's dark eyes blazing with feverish excitement.

'Did you see it … did you see the prophet's book written in strange hieroglyphics?'

Joshua shakes his head.

'I saw *nothing*! The shewing stone revealed nothing to me.'

Kelley groans as he starts to come round from his trance. He is groggy, like one awakened from a deep sleep.

'I need refreshment,' he murmurs.

Dee rushes to his side.

'Of course, good sir. I will have food brought up—'

The Skryer pushes him away. 'I will not eat in the presence of spirits,' he cries as he rises rather shakily to his feet. 'I will eat by your fire. Fresh water from your well, warm bread and honey on the honeycomb,' he commands as though Dee were his servant. 'Then I will rest,' the Skryer concludes.

The doctor's face falls in acute disappointment. Joshua thinks he looks like a child who's been given a wonderful Christmas present which is immediately snatched away from him.

'Are we done so soon?' Dee asks.

'If I am sufficiently restored, we will recommence at five o'clock this afternoon,' Kelley concludes in a voice that brooks no more questions.

The Skryer eats alone in complete silence then takes himself off to his room to rest. The minute he is out of sight, Mistress Dee rushes at her husband and clings onto him for dear life.

'Husband!' she cries out in a wild voice. 'The Skryer is evil! Send him hence – have him begone!' she implores.

'Hush, woman!' Dee chides her sharply. 'You will not offend an invited guest under my roof.'

'Nay, sir. Not so. I welcome all you invite into this house,' she answers in her own defence. 'Master Cross can bear me out ...' She stares at Joshua, who nods in agreement.

'You have treated me with great kindness, mistress,' he assures her.

'Edward Kelley is *not* a guest – he is a usurper,' she says in a voice that is low with fear. 'I spoke with the Skrying agent who brought him hither and departed after he partook of a bowl of broth with me. The agent told me that Kelley's right ear was lopped because he is a *forger* – he hath been tried by law and found guilty of forging coins and deeds of value. Husband, you have the largest library in England – nay Europe! It is stacked with books and ancient manuscripts, which this impostor may copy and sell on for a great profit.'

Doctor Dee looks genuinely shocked at this suggestion.

'Poppycock!' he cries, and makes to leave the room.

'Nay, husband!' Mistress Dee shouts as she runs after him. 'There is more.'

The doctor stops and turns to her. Joshua can see there is anger in his eyes – and fear too.

'His agent says he has other names. He is best known in the Skrying circle as Zoppo Magnus, but he changed to Edward Kelley when he moved from the north.'

'His name is irrelevant!' Dee protests. 'I am only concerned with what he can do for me.'

'Does that include necromancy, husband?' Mistress Dee whispers as she bends close to him. 'He called up Infernal Regiments at Sir Walter Raleigh's School of the Night.'

Dee angrily pushes his wife away from him.

'The agent told me that Kelley dug up the freshest corpses in a churchyard in Preston only last month to practise his necromancy on.'

'NO!' Doctor Dee shouts. 'The agent is a blathering fool. Sir Walter Raleigh sent Kelley hither with recommendations of his clear understanding, quick apprehension and excellent wit.'

'He is also sent hither because Raleigh's house is watched around the clock by Walsingham's spies,' his wife adds knowingly.

'He is welcome in this house as long as I say so,' Dee adds forcefully.

Mistress Dee breaks down and sobs.

'You promised me you would have no more Skryers! The last upset little Arthur with his evil eye – the boy had a fever for a week. The milk curdled in the churn, the hens stopped laying and I was sick with green bile for days after he'd gone.' She weeps as she makes the sign of the cross upon herself.

'Let no one see the sign of your Catholic faith,' Dee warns her. 'That single gesture puts my household at greater risk than any visit from a Skryer.'

And with that Dee turns his back on his wife, who

weeps uncontrollably at her husband's stubborn refusal to even consider her point of view.

With Joshua on his heels, Doctor Dee descends into the bowels of the house, down into the cellars to the inner sanctum of his Laboratory, where he slumps at his Alchemist's desk.

'I am privy to the knowledge that Kelley is a necromancer and hath changed his name,' Dee admits to the boy. 'I read it in his star chart long before he arrived.'

Joshua gapes at him in disbelief.

'So why did you put poor Mistress Dee through all that grief?'

'Because I will not be dissuaded from my course of action by a woman's hysterical fears.'

Joshua decides it's time to support the good lady of the house.

'To be honest, I don't like Edward Kelley either!' he admits. 'He makes you the servant and he the master. I didn't see anything in the shewing stone. Maybe it was all a hoax – a work of deceit,' he adds in Elizabethan speak.

Dee raises his head revealing his face, which is full of desperation.

'There was no deceit, Master Chai. You trust him not and therefore your heart is tight closed against him. I am *humbled* by his knowledge, my heart and mind are wide open to him. No medium has ever taken me thus far before. He summoned up Uriel, who will lead me to Michael, the warrior Archangel who threw Lucifer into eternal hellfire. Through Kelley I have access to Adam's Book – I can learn the language forged by God Himself!' Dee finishes in a voice shaking with emotion.

'If the Skrying agent spoke the truth to your wife then you could be putting your family at risk,' Joshua points out.

'Then I must take that risk,' says Dee firmly. 'I have wasted much time in the past on Skryers who were charlatans. You are a boy. You cannot comprehend how great is my need for this man Kelley.'

Stung to anger by his words, Joshua strongly protests.

'I may be a boy but I have knowledge of what evil can do! I was almost hounded to death by Leirtod, who chased me through the Underworld and across the River Styx.'

Momentarily distracted from the Skryer, the doctor stares at Joshua.

'Ah … so Lumaluce hid you in the past before, Master Chai?'

Joshua nods.

'He thought I would be safe in Ancient Greece, where I was protected by Heracles, Athene, Hermes, Apollo, Pythagoras and Socrates.'

'You met *Pythagoras*?' gasps the doctor.

'I was imprisoned with him in Athens. He spent the night explaining his theorem to me.'

'A great man, a *brilliant* mystic,' Dee enthuses.

Joshua doesn't say that he thinks Pythagoras is the

weirdest man he's ever met in his whole life! He simply nods and continues with his story.

'Even though I was protected by gods, scholars and heroes, Leirtod still tracked me down.' Joshua shivers as he recalls the terrors he lived through. 'It's *horrible* to be in fear of your life – as *you* might be if you join forces with this criminal who calls himself Edward Kelley.'

Dee shrugs.

'I am used to living with danger.'

Joshua clutches at the flowing sleeves of the doctor's red velvet gown.

'This is your *family*!' he exclaims. 'Is the lost Language of God worth the ruin of your wife and children?'

Dee slowly nods his head and replies in a grave voice, 'If he can unfold mysteries to me, I will follow Kelley to the ends of the earth.'

'But you could spend the rest of your life searching for something that might turn out to be a wild goose chase!' Joshua exclaims. 'Why not be happy with the riches that you already possess? Your astrological charts, your scientific research, your library, your position at court, your children. Surely that's enough for any man?'

'Aye, any man but I!' Dee replies. 'Zoppo Magnus will open doors to me that have previously been locked. I must follow him, Master Chai – it is my destiny.'

Joshua sighs heavily. Further argument would be a waste of time. Doctor Dee, the most brilliant scholar in England, has made up his mind to follow his Skryer into the unknown … and Joshua knows that for the moment at least he too must follow wherever the man with the lopped-off ear will lead them.

Meanwhile, Dido is on the move! Restless with Hampton Court, which Thomasina tells Dido holds bad childhood memories for the Queen, Elizabeth and her retinue are headed for the Palace of Whitehall.

Dido's in a panic! How will Joshua know where to find her? How can she tell him where the court is bound and how does she know how long the Queen will choose to stay at Whitehall?

'Her Majesty has a restless spirit,' says Dido as she and Thomasina are commissioned by Lady Blanche Parry, Mistress of the Robes, to take out the clothes chest and pack up the Queen's five hundred dresses.

Thomasina answers her from behind a pile of heavy Spanish farthingales, which are lined with rope or stiffened with bent willow to give them the rigid shape the Queen so favours for her flowing overskirts.

'How will Doctor Dee know the Queen's whereabouts?' Dido asks Thomasina.

'Speak plainly, Dorothea. You are more concerned with his pupil Master Chai than the good doctor,' teases Thomasina. 'Be assured the Queen sends word of her whereabouts to her Conjuror before she notifies the court of her departure. He is always the first to know where she is. If he does not call upon her soon at Whitehall, she will no doubt call upon him at Mortlake.'

'It would be nice to accompany the Queen there – and see the doctor's library,' says Dido.

'Ay. 'Tis a fine sight – as are his Observatory and Laboratory,' Thomasina replies.

Lady Blanche bustles in and chivvies them crossly.

'Go to! Go to and tarry not!' she snaps. 'You have barely commenced your duties and the Queen expects us this very night at the Palace of Whitehall for revels.'

'Ma'am,' protests Thomasina. 'We arrived at Hampton Court with clothes chests enough for five hundred gowns; now the Queen hath added another thirty to her wardrobe.'

Lady Blanche's tired face looks even more fatigued.

'Aye ...' she murmurs. 'I had forgot the dressmaker she brought over from France.'

'He made her woollen kirtles with embroidered foreparts for hunting, with leather shoes, hats and belts to match,' Thomasina reminds Lady Blanche.

'Aye ... and sleeves and shirts too,' Lady Blanche recalls.

'And she hath added to her wardrobe a number of low-cut French gowns with matching petticoats and kirtles of velvet embroidered with seed pearls,' Dido points out.

'We must cram them all into the clothes chests,' urges the Mistress of the Robes.

'We cannot cram in gowns finished off with seed pearls

and gems!' cries Thomasina in horror. 'They will crush and spoil and the Queen will have us horsewhipped.

'I have not time to commission the making of new clothes chests,' snaps Lady Blanche. 'Do your best and let the servants carry what remains. Now I must attend to Her Majesty's jewellery or she will arrive at Whitehall without a tiara to her head!'

Lady Blanche bustles out of the Privy Chambers leaving Thomasina to pack a sea of smocks, bodices, corsets, petticoats, shirts, ruffs, wigs, shoes, ribbons, nets and an assortment of small padded crescents that Dido has never seen before. 'They are "rowles" to go about Her Majesty's waist to add a swing to her heavy skirts,' Thomasina explains.

'It is a wonder the Queen can put one foot in front of another,' says Dido as she examines a pair of soft leather slippers with a high wedged heel. 'She's so tightly corseted she can barely breathe. Her farthingales are so heavy with wood and rope she can hardly walk, and her shoes are so high she can barely stand – and she paints her face with white lead which will finally kill her. And all for the sake of vanity!'

'The Queen is indeed vain,' Thomasina says as she sorts out pairs of expensive silk knitted hose imported from Belgium. 'But mark me, Dorothea. She dresses richly not only for her own delight but because she uses any situation to her political advantage – and rich gowns *always* impress. The fabrics and jewels she flaunts convey wealth, power and prestige. You will shortly hear the people on our travels about the country, Dorothea. They call out, "Queen Bess, the goddess!" Or they cry, "Queen of Heaven!" as she passes them by, dazzling them with her rich array. Elizabeth dresses the part – she dresses to *impress!*' says Thomasina with a knowing smile.

Their conversation is interrupted by Bess Throckmorton, who dashes in and throws herself into a carved oak chair, where she sits panting to get her breath back.

'Bess!' cries Thomasina in alarm. 'What has happened?'

'Haven't you heard?' Bess gasps.

Dido and Thomasina shake their heads.

'Sir Walter Raleigh has been arrested by Walsingham! Raleigh is in the Tower of London awaiting trial.'

'For *what*?' demands Thomasina.

'Treasonable deeds,' Bess answers as she runs to the door of the Privy Chamber and peers out. Seeing nobody there, she quickly closes the door and hurries back. 'Rumour hath it that Raleigh has been arrested because of his unsavoury connections with the School of the Night.'

Terrified of being overheard, Bess drops her voice to the merest whisper. 'He hath been arrested for *witchcraft!*'

— 8 —
ARCHANGEL

Doctor Dee is delighted to see Kelley rise from his bed and announce that he will resume their skrying session.

'Oh, thank you, good sir, thank you,' the doctor says in a meek grovelling voice that irritates Joshua.

'I would pray excuse myself from your skrying,' Joshua whispers to Dee when Kelley is out of the room.

'Nay, Master Chai!' the doctor exclaims. 'I have use of you.'

'But I can't *see* anything, nor *hear* anything,' Joshua protests. 'What use can I be?'

'I need you by me to record everything that passes,' Dee tells him. 'In my excitement I may not recall details of significance. Can you write?' he asks suddenly.

'Of course I can write!' Joshua replies indignantly.

'Then you shall be my scribe, Master Chai!' exclaims Dee. 'You shall pen all that I say and all that I see.'

'But I don't want to be there, in the session,' Joshua answers mutinously. 'It scares me,' he adds reluctantly.

Dee eyes him thoughtfully.

'You think the Skryer will summon up your enemy, Leirtod?'

Joshua nods his head. The doctor pats him solemnly on the shoulder and answers in a warm reassuring voice.

'Have no fear, Master Chai. I will protect you.'

And so the three of them sit once more around the shewing stone in Doctor Dee's Observatory. The doctor has placed a roll of parchment and a quill pen in an inkpot before Joshua, who gapes at the quill in disbelief.

'Is this a joke?' he laughs.

Dee does not return his smile.

'I jest not. I would have you record the events that take place in this room,' he answers in a stern voice.

'But I can't write with a FEATHER!'

''Tis a feather with a fashioned nib on the end – now go to, sir. The Skryer hath not all day to waste,' snaps the doctor.

Joshua takes the quill pen from the pot and immediately blobs ink all over the crackly parchment paper.

'Just don't talk fast,' he warns the doctor. 'I don't do shorthand!'

In nervous fascination, Joshua watches Kelley's eyes reflect the milky white of the crystals in the stone, and then his face goes slack and limp as he slips into a strange trance-like state. Minutes later, Doctor Dee clutches the edge of his desk and stares raptly into the shewing stone at images that are certainly not evident to Joshua. As the words fall from the Skryer's and the doctor's mouths,

Joshua writes them down as best he can in an inky sprawling hand.

'You must construct a Holy Table such as the one in the glass,' Kelley chants in his melodic skrying voice. 'Construct it from sweet wood and stand each leg on a divine seal inscribed with a cross set within a circle. On this Holy Table Michael the Archangel will inscribe the letters from Enoch's alphabet.'

'He will teach me the language of God?' gasps Dee.

'He will impart it through me, your faithful Skryer,' Kelley tells him.

'Hah! The image is changing,' cries the doctor.

Joshua glances up from his writing to see the crystals churn but nothing more. Dee, however, beholds an image so bright he has to cover his eyes against it.

'The light burns!' the doctor cries, then slowly he drops his arms and smiles in wonder. 'I see *him* ...' he whispers. 'His wings are golden and he carries a sword.' Dee's face is transformed with joy. 'Ah ... 'tis Michael the Archangel!'

'Hush! Michael would speak with you,' says Kelley. 'Harken to the words God gave to Adam and repeat them well.'

Doctor Dee leans closer to the shewing stone. His brow furrows as he listens hard, then he makes a sequence of bizarre sounds, the likes of which Joshua has never heard before – and he certainly can't write them down with a quill pen that sprays black ink onto his fingers!

'*Arnay vah nol gadeth adney ox vals neth gemseh ah orza val gemah, oh gedva on zembah nohhad vomfah olden,*' mumbles Dee.

Kelley too takes up the litany, which he chants in his melodic skrying voice almost sending Joshua into a trance too. He tries his best to write down the strange words that he hardly knows how to spell! Suddenly the doctor lurches towards the stone, which he only just manages to stop himself from grasping hold of.

'Ahh … behold the first man and woman!' he says with trembling reverence.

'Adam and Eve naked in their innocence,' Kelley murmurs. 'Uncorrupted by the Fall – before their expulsion from Paradise.'

'Hark!' Doctor Dee cries. 'They are speaking the words God taught them!' Dee starts to chant the strange words again. '*Arnay vah nol gadeth adney ox vals neth gemseh ah orza val gemah, oh gedva …*'

Joshua briefly stops writing to watch the doctor, who is filled with emotion. Tears course down his cheeks as he sits transfixed by the images in the stone which Joshua *cannot* see. Joshua sighs. How can he be *sure* that the doctor is seeing the things he says he's seeing? How can he be certain that Dee isn't hallucinating or, worse still, being duped by Kelley? And why has *he*, Joshua, agreed to write down the entire incident when he can't see anything? Feeling irritated with himself, Joshua throws down the quill pen with such force a flying blob of ink lands right on the end of his nose! Just as Joshua's wondering where he can find a rag to clean himself, he sees Edward Kelley go as stiff as a board. His face is no longer flaccid and pale – it is rigid with terror. Joshua turns to glance into the stone, which Kelley cannot take his eyes off, and he too stiffens with terror. Now he *can* see something. In the swirling crystals a face emerges … it is the malevolent image of Leirtod!

'AHHH! He is here!' screams Kelley, and rises so quickly from his chair that it falls over and clatters onto the wooden floor behind him. 'Your house is haunted by the evil one, Doctor Dee!'

The Skryer lurches at Joshua and grabs his shoulder so tightly the boy yelps in pain.

'OW!'

In his fear the Skryer has thrown off his cowled hood, revealing the livid scar that has healed over the place where his ear once was.

'Leirtod seeks to destroy this boy that you protect! He has followed him from a far place and comes between you and the Book of Adam!'

As Kelley speaks, the crystals in the shewing stone darken into two pinpoints of pulsing hatred which Joshua immediately recognises as Leirtod's vengeful eyes. His heart thumps so violently in his ribcage it feels like it might burst.

'You must expel Leirtod immediately!' cries the Skryer in a frenzy. 'If he remains, all the Archangels will take flight and no more will be revealed to you. You must burn him out tonight, Doctor Dee – expunge him from this house with fire and brimstone!'

Kelley's ravings suddenly cease. He turns pale and falls to the ground, limp with exhaustion.

'I can do no more … I am emptied out,' he groans feebly. 'Tell Mistress Dee to prepare me meat and wine, then I will rest.' The Skryer turns to Joshua with eyes full of foreboding. '*He* is come for you,' he whispers to Joshua, who is shaking with terror. 'You must banish Leirtod, Doctor Dee … or the boy will surely die.'

With Edward Kelley firmly established at the kitchen table, served by Mistress Dee who looks distinctly nervous, Doctor Dee sets off for his Observatory holding a jar of brimstone to his chest.

'I need you, Joshua,' he calls out. 'I cannot exorcise Leirtod alone.'

Joshua follows reluctantly with anger burning in him like a slow fuse. *WHY* did the doctor allow Edward Kelley into his home, seethes Joshua. The Skryer has upset Mistress Dee and her children, he's transformed the doctor into a doting fool and now he's summoned up Leirtod, who Joshua knows will haunt Mortlake until he tracks down his prey. Emboldened by his anger, Joshua blurts out, 'You may part with your soul if you follow Edward Kelley!'

Dee whirls round on Joshua with his eyes flashing angrily.

'My soul belongs to Christ and no other!' he shouts.

'The Skryer has brought evil into your house,' Joshua cries before he can check himself.

Dee glares at him.

'Nay, Master Chai,' he answers in a low angry voice. 'It is you that Leirtod pursues … *it is you* that hath brought evil hence.'

Fighting back tears of fear, Joshua replies, 'I trusted you, sir, when you promised to protect me. Instead you have put me at risk … and I am sore afraid,' he ends, as he brushes tears from his eyes. Stung by his words, the doctor seizes a candlestick in which a lighted taper burns and walks purposefully towards the door.

'Come,' he calls out. 'Let us cleanse this house of evil.'

They enter the Observatory, where Doctor Dee pours the brimstone into bowls, then sets fire to it with a candle flame. The smell is gaggingly nauseating!

'It's sulphur!' Joshua cries, as he covers his mouth. 'Ugh! It stinks!'

In the dark, holding the bowls of burning brimstone, they hurry down the long oak-panelled corridor that leads to the library. Joshua shivers as he feels a chill upon his back. He does not know whether it is the sudden chill of evening or fear that makes his skin creep.

In the gable end of the house that forms the entrance to the library, Doctor Dee has had built an enormous stained glass window which depicts Christ's crucifixion. Joshua's eyes lift towards it ... and his heart heaves up into his throat. Bathed in the light from the setting sun slanting through the jewel colours of the window is *Leirtod*! His gaunt white face is momentarily coloured ruby red so that it looks like it is running with blood. He doesn't say a word, but his eyes drill into Joshua's skull as if he would destroy him. Doctor Dee quickly stands between Leirtod and the boy.

'Get thee hence, son of Lucifer!' he cries fearlessly.

Leirtod's image drifts out of the high window and like a dark cloud he descends, his evil face twisted into a mocking leer.

'Thou wouldst take me for a fool, doctor?' He laughs a hard laugh that seems to rake the back of his throat. 'I have dwelled too long in hell to fear fire.'

He passes through the cloying smoke that Doctor Dee wafts before him. 'Let us talk of your Skryer, Zoppo Magnus, who has recently joined our brethren.'

Doctor Dee visibly starts at the mention of his Skryer's real name.

'Ah ... you did not know that Zoppo is one of the Infernal Regiment and enjoys with us the Black Ceremonies of the Night?'

'He has sold his soul to Satan!' gasps the doctor.

'He was obliged to in order to gain knowledge that would otherwise have been inaccessible to him,' Leirtod replies. 'He still remains a third-rate Skryer who has you in his thrall. He will run you ragged with his whims and fancies – and he will claim your wife.'

Leirtod smiles a wicked, knowing smile. Then he bends and whispers into Dee's ear, 'I know the innermost secrets of your heart, Conjuror. You would trade all you possess in exchange for the Philosopher's Stone. Your desire to turn base metal into gold and transform dead matter into living tissue will have you play God just as I once did.'

Inflamed with anger, Doctor Dee cries out, 'Nay, not I, son of Satan! I would sooner take my own life than quench the life of Lumaluce as you once sought to do.'

'Lumaluce stole *my* brilliance!' Leirtod rages.

'You were jealous of him so you conspired to cast him into eternal darkness – but your plan failed. It was YOU who was driven out whilst he triumphed!'

'Fear not, doctor. I will triumph over Lumaluce yet. I will have my revenge through his silver-eyed boy. His father will cry out in agony when I present him with the corpse of his favoured son.'

Trembling with fear, Joshua presses himself into the folds of Dee's flowing velvet gown.

'You will not touch the boy while I live and breathe,' whispers the doctor through gritted teeth.

'Then you will die together, Conjuror!'

With a venomous smile, Leirtod brandishes his silver dagger. As they cower away from the glinting blade, something wonderful happens. The stained glass Angel hovering over the head of the dying Christ suddenly blazes rays down onto Doctor Dee and Joshua, who are instantly drenched in a golden glow that repels Leirtod! Screaming in frustration, he continues to slash at them with his knife, but he makes no impact. Joshua gazes in wonder at the Angel, who is now standing outside the window, looking down on them. His long golden wings beat the air as beams from his body burn into Leirtod, who drops the knife as if it were scalding him. When he bends to retrieve it, the Angel's rays catch the blade, which melts into a pool of liquid silver. In a frenzy of hatred, Leirtod charges at Joshua. His hands are raised as if to grab him around the neck and strangle the life out of his body. Doctor Dee bravely puts himself between Joshua and Leirtod, but the golden glow cocoons both of them from Leirtod, who simply cannot touch them.

'Aaaaagh!' he roars in rage, as the angelic beams burn brighter.

Blinded and terrified of the increasing light, Leirtod swirls his black cloak about his face and is gone. The glow around Doctor Dee and Joshua disperses like a warm mist. As they step free of it, they see that the Angel has taken up his position once more in the stained glass window and has eyes only for his dying Lord.

'Do you think the Angel that saved us was Uriel?' Joshua whispers incredulously.

'Methinks he was an angel sent by your father to guard you,' says Doctor Dee thoughtfully. 'We are not alone in this fight,' he adds as he lays a hand on Joshua's shoulder. 'Come, Master Chai, we must enter my library and cleanse it swiftly.'

By the time they've fumigated the library, the Observatory and the Laboratory, it is nearly midnight. Joshua is exhausted but he is also afraid of sleeping alone in his pitch-dark bedchamber. Seeing the boy's frightened expression, Doctor Dee suggests he sleeps in the closet beside his own bedchamber. Joshua readily agrees, but sleep doesn't come easily. The memory of Leirtod's slashing knife has him tossing and turning on his straw mattress. Tomorrow there will be more dealings with Zoppo Magnus. Joshua prays that the doctor will ask less of the Skryer, but he knows in his heart that Dee's appetite for Adam's Book and the Philosopher's Stone is insatiable. Joshua dreads what further secrets the Skryer might unfold and what dark spirits he might disturb in the process ...

⟶ 9 ⟵
THE PALACE
OF WHITEHALL

Dido's journey by river to the Palace of Whitehall is swift and pleasant, apart from a decomposing corpse they row by.

'UGH!' she screams, at the sight of the badly mutilated face, but Thomasina hardly bats an eyelid.

'Most likely a common villain caught up in a street brawl,' she muses as the corpse drifts past her.

Dido averts her eyes and fastens them firmly upon the black and white timbered houses with high gables that line the waterfront. She gasps in surprise when their boat breasts a sharp bend and the Palace of Whitehall appears, spread-eagled over acres of land butting onto the river.

'It looks more like a village than a palace!' Dido exclaims.

'Aye, 'tis an impressive sight and grand to boot,' says Thomasina. 'There is a thoroughfare the size of a street running through the heart of the palace from Holbein Gate to King Street. The Queen's Privy Council meet in those chambers yonder,' she says, pointing to a suite of rooms with large latticed bay windows that overlook the river.

'The Queen's Privy Chamber faces the Council Chamber, so there is little privacy from the royal advisors during the Queen's sojourn at Whitehall. We are constantly disturbed by my Lords Hatton, Burghley, Cecil and Walsingham. Forsooth, even when we walk with the Queen in her Privy Garden, her statesmen approach and besiege her with questions.'

'Does Sir Francis Walsingham have his spies here?' Dido asks nervously.

'Aye, Dorothea. He goes nowhere, at home nor abroad, without them!' Thomasina exclaims.

'I wish Walsingham were in foreign lands so that the Queen might smile favourably on Sir Walter Raleigh,' says Bess Throckmorton, who is perched precariously between two vast clothes chests. ''Tis only her Secretary of State that keeps Raleigh locked up in the tower.'

'I fancy you carry a flame for Sir Walter ...?' teases Lady Mary Sydney.

Bess blushes prettily.

'He has the shapeliest calves of any man in court,' she replies with a girlish giggle.

'And he has the favour of the Queen!' says Thomasina sharply.

'Fiddle-dee!' exclaims Bess. 'The Queen favours so many: Sir Christopher Hatton, Sir Francis Drake ... her beloved Robert Dudley. Surely she can spare Sir Walter Raleigh?'

'Do not play with fire,' says Thomasina in a voice that

is dark with foreboding. 'The Queen would *sorely* miss him.'

The Mistress of the Robes chivvies the Ladies of the Bedchamber in the long tedious business of unpacking all the dresses, petticoats, corsets, farthingales, smocks, ruffs, wigs, stocking and shoes from the clothes chests, which are so many they make a pile that nearly reaches the elaborately worked ceiling of the royal bedroom.

'The Queen may dress to impress, but she certainly doesn't travel light,' says Dido as she shakes out the Queen's many wigs and places them on stands so that their bright red curls and clusters of waves may drop out of their creases. 'Oh, no!' she gasps when she sees that one of the wigs is running with head lice. Without a second's hesitation, Dido throws the offending wig out of the window into the river below. 'Ugh, disgusting!' she exclaims.

Lady Blanche stares at the new Lady of the Bedchamber as if she would hit her.

'Retrieve it immediately!' she cries in fury.

'I can't!' protests Dido. 'It's crawling with enormous head lice … and anyway it's sunk into the river,' she adds nervously.

'You'll sink into the river if you repeat such a deed,' scolds the Mistress of the Robes. 'A sprinkling with talcum powder would have cleansed the wig of impurities.' Dido can't believe her ears.

'Head lice spread like wild fire! They have to be destroyed before they infect everybody,' she protests.

'The Queen is crawling with head lice!' exclaims Lady

Blanche. 'Most of the court suffer the same condition. It is better in the winter months when the frost kills them off, but in the warmer months they multiply and plague us all. Her majesty will surely miss that wig for it matched her Flanders gown of black satin with the gold embroidered stomacher.'

As Lady Blanche fusses and bemoans her fate if the Queen should hear that her best wig is sunk to the bottom of the Thames, Dido puts a hand up to her head and starts to scratch her suddenly itchy scalp.

'Have I got lice?' she asks as she bends her head to Thomasina for inspection.

The little maid scans Dido's abundant red curls.

'Not yet,' she answers. 'But forsooth you soon shall have!'

Dido, Thomasina, Lady Mary Sydney and Bess Throck-morton are thrown into a panic when Lady Blanche hurries in and announces that the Queen is back from riding and will change from her riding clothes into a fresh gown.

'She hath a meeting with her Privy Council and the French Ambassador who is come to speak on behalf of the Duke of Anjou,' says Lady Blanche, who is pink with rushing about. 'Lay out the Venetian gown of crimson velvet and the russet satin cut low at the front in the French fashion.'

As the Ladies of the Bedchamber dash to and fro finding

velvet sleeves, embroidered kirtles, weighty farthingales, shirts, petticoats, bum rolls and corsets, Lady Blanche sets out the Queen's ornate make-up. Dido watches her in rapt fascination ... Firstly, Lady Blanche mixes white lead and vinegar paste that she will apply to the Queen's face, neck and bosom. This will then be covered with uncooked egg white combined with talcum powder to give a smooth even gloss and cover up any pockmarks, scars, freckles or wrinkles – of which the Queen has many! Vermilion will be applied to the royal cheeks and lips, and belladonna will be dropped in the royal eye to give it a fine sparkle. Her Majesty's eyebrows will be plucked to the finest whisper of an arch and so will her hairline. Dido winced when she first saw Lady Blanche plucking the Queen's forehead! Thomasina told her that a high brow was a sure sign of aristocracy and thus the Queen suffered the torture of having her brow plucked by a whole inch to create a fashionably high forehead. Dido thanked her lucky stars that she had no aspirations to join the royal aristocracy!

As Lady Blanche and Mary Sydney prepare the Queen for her Privy Council, the other Ladies of the Bedchamber are allowed out into the Privy Garden for a breath of fresh air. In a sunny bower they sit together on a stone bench, where Bess Throckmorton continues to rattle on about Sir Walter Raleigh, who she's clearly besotted by.

'It was the Skryer's doing that sent him to jail,' she says crossly. 'Sir Walter hired one such from Lancashire because he hath great skills for calling up the dead.'

'Who told you so?' asks Thomasina sharply.

'His page boy, who I gave gold to,' Bess replies with a giggle. 'Now I know *everything* about Sir Walter,' she announces with unashamed pride. 'Even down to his School of the Night!'

'Ssshh!' hisses Thomasina. 'Walsingham's spies are *everywhere*. This very morning I saw Ingram Frizar lurking here in the Privy Garden.'

'What *are* you two talking about?' puzzles Dido.

'We must walk about,' Thomasina insists. 'If Bess is to speak carelessly, let it be in the open with no bushes close by where Ingram Frizar can hide and eavesdrop on our conversation.'

They obey the little maid and walk down the wide thoroughfare that leads to Holbein Gate, where they can see all who approach from a good distance.

'You have not heard of a Skryer, Dorothea?' Bess asks in amazement.

Dido shakes her head.

'It is a medium,' Thomasina says in a voice that is cold with disapproval.

'A Skryer makes his living by calling up spirits,' Bess whispers in a voice that is half frightened and half excited by such a prospect.

'It is foolish nonsense and dangerous to boot,'

Thomasina adds. 'The Secretary of State is fiercely against such practices – as is the Queen herself!'

'But Sir Walter Raleigh told me that *everybody* does it in private,' Bess says with a giggle. 'All the gentlemen of the court have Skryers in their pay, and ladies too. It's very fashionable. Some say the Queen herself has visited a Skryer in secret.'

'Bess, hush your foolish mouth!' cries Thomasina. 'The Queen is head of the Church in England – why would she seek out demonic practices? It would damn her soul and her reputation.'

'Mayhap she's a mind to find out through a medium who it would be wisest to wed,' Bess teases. 'Philip of Spain or the Duke of Anjou … or maybe her bonny Lord Dudley!'

Thomasina shakes her head at Bess' foolishness.

'If your father did not hold a high office at court you would soon be banished for your effrontery,' she chides.

'Who is this Skryer who hath caused so much trouble?' Dido persists.

'Why, you saw him yourself,' Bess remarks. 'He was in the rose garden while Sir Walter sat and wooed the Queen with sweet love verses.' Bess' pretty face falls into a sulky expression. 'He penned those for me, but read them to her!' she adds crossly.

Dido ignores Bess' grievances and asks another question.

'Do you mean the man who wore a cowled hood like a monk and had a severed ear?'

'The very one. Master Edward Kelley from the parish of Preston in Lancashire. Sir Walter said he was most excellent and called up demons and angels to his School of the Night.'

Thomasina shivers and hurries ahead of babbling Bess.

'Oh, I am afeared when you speak so, lady!' she exclaims. 'Why would anyone as clever and favoured as Sir Walter want to consult with *devils*?'

'I know full well why,' Bess replies with a smug smile. 'Sir Walter says we are ignorant – limited by boundaries which we should push at and look beyond.' Bess' pretty face wrinkles as if she has trouble keeping up with the concepts which Raleigh put to her. 'He says there is a science in the stars and the movements of the planets ...'

Thomasina raises her pale green eyes as if to say, you consider this is *new*!

'It is not the study of the stars and the planets that troubles me,' Thomasina tells Bess. 'It is Raleigh's dangerous interest in the occult.'

'Walter tells me 'tis another science, just as unexplored and exciting as the science of astrology. He says the mysteries of the dark side are as unfathomable as those in the deepest depths of the ocean,' Bess ends with a romantic tremor in her earnest voice.

'God's Bones!' seethes Thomasina. 'He talks fiddlesticks and you forsooth do believe every word that drops from his lips. He dabbles in *Black Magic* and necromancy, you foolish, witless maid! If Raleigh is caught with the Skryer he will linger longer in the Tower than he reckoned!'

Bess' blue eyes blaze with anger.

'I am neither witless nor foolish. I know *where* Sir Walter sent Edward Kelley for protection,' she says with a sly smile.

Thomasina shrugs. 'Why would I care where the Skryer tarries?' she answers dismissively.

'You will care when I tell you that he is hiding under the roof of your precious Doctor Dee,' Bess replies with a smirk on her face. She gets satisfaction as she sees the colour drain away from Thomasina's face.

'He is in Mortlake?' she gasps.

'With Joshua?' squeaks Dido fearfully.

'Aye …' Bess answers slowly, savouring her moment of self-importance. 'Sir Walter Raleigh cannot be so great a fool else the good doctor would not have opened his door to the Skryer he sent. What say you now, Miss Thomasina?'

The little maid says nothing, but puts a hand to her face and walks away from her friends as if deeply disturbed.

Dido rebukes Bess.

'You should not worry her so,' she says.

'Fie, she should not mock me so!' snaps Bess, and with a swirl of her richly embroidered satin skirts she walks off in the direction of Holbein Gate.

Dido catches up with Thomasina, who is walking as quickly as her little legs will take her.

'What ails you?' Dido asks.

'If the Secretary of State has had the Skryer followed, then Doctor Dee and Joshua will be in grave danger. Raleigh is in the Tower as an example to all – it is against the law to hold skrying sessions.'

'Could Doctor Dee and Joshua be imprisoned too?' gasps Dido.

Thomasina nods her head and continues to walk along the path.

'Raleigh must have sent Edward Kelley to Doctor Dee so that he could protect him while Raleigh languishes like the vapid fool he is in the Tower.' Thomasina sighs as she slumps onto one of the stone benches on the footpath. 'For sure Walsingham will have had Kelley watched … I would wager ten golden guineas that Ingram Frizar has been prowling the grounds of Durham House these last weeks.'

'So Walsingham's spies will follow Edward Kelley to Mortlake and arrest the Skryer, the doctor and anybody else colluding with them?' Dido cries.

'Ssshh!' Thomasina hisses. 'Lest you want all to know your business.'

Dido drops onto the bench beside Thomasina.

'Our friends could be arrested and sent to the Tower,' Thomasina says in a terrified whisper.

Dido takes hold of her small hand and grips it firmly in her own.

'Oh, Thomasina … if only we could warn them!'

~ 10 ~
FITS OF TEMPER

Unaware of the fate of Sir Walter Raleigh languishing in the Tower of London, Joshua at Mortlake is trying his best to soothe the frayed nerves of Mistress Dee, who he encounters on his way to the dining hall.

'Joshua,' she whispers as she urgently pulls him aside. 'This Skryer is exploiting my good husband with his wicked nature and abominable lies.'

Joshua shifts awkwardly. He's a guest under this woman's roof but she's confiding in him like he's one of the family. Joshua has no choice but to speak to her quite frankly.

'Doctor Dee won't turn out Kelley until he has revealed all of his secrets.'

'That could take *years*!' she cries in distress. 'And all the while the Skryer sits at my table and treats me like his serving wench. Joshua, I am choleric with stomach pains and vomiting while he remains in my house.'

Joshua tries to lift the mood.

'Maybe he'll get bored and move back to court,' he says hopefully.

'Nay, he will not do that while he has access to my husband's library.' She lowers her voice to such a whisper

Joshua has to bend down to catch what she's saying. 'My husband should look to his rare manuscripts which may well go missing.'

Joshua stares at her with wide eyes.

'Do you *really* think Kelley is a thief and a forger?'

'Aye, for sure. The punishment for forging is the lopping off of the right ear. You can see it with your own eyes!' Mistress Dee exclaims. 'There is more to tell, Joshua. I sent one of the servant lads after the Skrying agent, who in exchange for money gave forth further information.' She nervously covers her mouth with her hand so that not even the walls can hear what she has to impart. 'Edward Kelley was *Father Kelley* in the diocese of Preston, Lancashire – he is a priest on the run!'

Joshua gasps as he realises the grave danger the Mortlake household is in.

'Harbouring a priest is a treasonable offence punishable by death!' Mistress Dee adds, with a frightened sob in her voice.

'I think the doctor may know more of Kelley's history than he lets on to you,' Joshua says in an attempt to reassure her.

'Aye, mayhap … but my husband tells me *nought*,' she says with bitter finality. Taking a deep breath, she grimly adds, 'I had best return to my duties – and serve Master Kelley the food he has ordered.'

Kelley sits at the dining table in a truculent mood.

'I slept badly,' he says sourly. 'Your house is cold and draughty, Doctor Dee, and too many owls inhabit your garden.'

Joshua covers his mouth to stop himself from bursting out laughing. What a drama queen Kelley is! Complaining about the presence of evil spirits is one thing, but grumbling about hooting owls is *ridiculous*! What's the doctor supposed to do … ? Go out and shoot them with his crossbow!

After a large bowl of porridge thickly laced with cream and honey, Kelley is persuaded to do another skrying session.

'And then I shall take myself off to your library, where I will study your charts and manuscripts at my leisure,' he tells Dee rather than asks him.

As the doctor bows in agreement, Mistress Dee exchanges an anxious look with Joshua, which Kelley is quick to notice.

'Speak plain, lady. Do you resent my request?' he asks sharply.

'Nay, sir,' she answers calmly. 'Know you either Greek or Latin?'

Kelley moodily shakes his head.

'Then *how* will you read the manuscripts? Without the knowledge of Greek and Latin you will find them incomprehensible.'

The doctor glares at his wife and quickly says, 'My

good wife is too loose with her tongue. She omits to mention I have many books written in English.'

'Your good wife bears a grudge,' Kelley remarks darkly.

'Mistress Dee will do as she's told,' snaps the doctor and pushing back his chair he leaves the room followed by Kelley, who looks back at the lady of the house with a self-satisfied smirk on his scarred face.

Joshua, Doctor Dee and Kelley gather in the Observatory, which is loud with the sound of rain falling against the mullioned windowpanes. Kelley shivers as he sits hunched before the shewing stone, which this time takes much longer to reveal its secrets. As Joshua waits expectantly, he sees Kelley press his right hand to his temple. He sweats profusely and starts to shake as he strains to summon spirits to the table. Slowly he relaxes into a trance and his eyes reflect the churning milky white crystals in the stone. Hardly daring to breathe, Doctor Dee presses himself closer to the table.

'What can you see?' Joshua whispers.

The doctor shakes his head and looks mystified. He bends his head closer to the glass and squints his eyes as if he were trying to make out something small.

'It is a map drawn on an ancient scroll,' he mutters.

'It is marked with strange objects and is written in an unfathomable language ...' Kelley interrupts the doctor. 'Follow the map and you will find the Philosopher's

Stone,' he chants melodically as he rocks back and forth in his chair.

Dee grips Joshua's hand so tightly his nails bite into the boy's skin and draw blood.

'*The Philosopher's Stone,*' he gasps.

'It is hid in the secret of the deep,' Kelley mumbles. 'In the vaults where Joseph, who lent the tomb from which Christ our Saviour rose, now lies.'

Joshua is utterly bewildered by Kelley's words – *who*'s Joseph and *where* is his tomb? Doctor Dee has no problem in understanding.

'Joseph of Arimathea lent his tomb to Jesus,' he mutters.

'The mighty hand of God is upon thee, Doctor Dee!' the Skryer exclaims. 'Seek hard and thou shalt have the Stone!'

Suppressing his excitement, Dee gently presses Kelley for more details.

'*How* shall I claim this holy thing?'

'You must dig deep in sanctified earth.'

'*Where* shall I dig?' whispers the doctor.

'In the birthplace of English Christendom – the final resting place of King Arthur.'

Unable to control his delight, Doctor Dee gives an ecstatic cry.

'GLASTONBURY!'

Kelley frowns as if disturbed by the noise, then he continues.

'Adam's Book, the Scroll and the Stone belong to you,' he says. 'They are your destiny.'

And there the trance ends. Kelley slumps forward, exhausted by his efforts, and all is silent, apart from the rain falling against the leaded windowpanes. Doctor Dee turns to Joshua, his eyes ablaze with joy.

'The Book of Adam and the Philosopher's Stone belong to *ME*!' he cries. 'When my Skryer has taught me the language of God I shall be able to read the map and find the Philosopher's Stone!' he announces with a triumphant ring in his voice. 'Master Chai, this is indeed wondrous and marvellous to mine ear!'

As the words pour out of Doctor Dee's mouth, Joshua's heart sinks as he realises that in delivering this latest promise Kelley has guaranteed himself a place in Doctor Dee's household for as long as it takes the doctor to learn the lost language of God. *Only* the Skryer can reveal the alphabet to him. *Only* the Skryer can help him decipher the map and *only* the Skryer can lead the doctor to the Philosopher's Stone. Kelley's ingeniously manipulative plot is crystal clear to Joshua and Mistress Dee, but Doctor Dee, the cleverest man in England, is blissfully ignorant of the scheming mind behind it. He is *bewitched*. With a shiver Joshua recalls Leirtod's words from the previous night: *Zoppo Magnus has the doctor in his thrall*! Joshua desperately wants to say something, to warn the doctor, but Kelley stirs and whatever words Joshua might have spoken are stopped in his mouth.

'I must fortify my spirit,' Kelley announces. 'Tell Mistress Dee to bring milk, bread and honey to the library,' he instructs.

Doctor Dee rushes to his side.

'I will bring the food myself, sir,' he says as he takes Kelley by the arm and gently guides him out of the Observatory. 'We have much to speak of,' he adds excitedly. 'The secret you have revealed to me today gives me great joy. No words can express my gratitude ...'

Joshua doesn't follow them into the library: he certainly doesn't want to watch Doctor Dee humble himself even further before Zoppo Magnus!

Queen Elizabeth returns in a filthy temper from her meeting with her Privy Council and the French Ambassador.

'Madam, I implore you,' says Walsingham as he scuttles in her imperious wake. 'Consider the Duke of Anjou ... it would be so propitious a marriage—'

He gets no further. Elizabeth slams the door in his face then turns to her Mistress of the Robes and yells, 'Let not the Master Spy come hither into my private chambers!'

Lady Blanche curtsies and presses her back to the door as if she would stop a herd of charging bull elephants. Elizabeth turns on her startled Ladies of the Bedchamber.

'Dorothea! Bring me my riding habit!' As Dido scuttles off to find the clothes the Queen demands, Bess Throckmorton is instructed to go and find Lord Dudley.

'Tell him to prepare to ride out with me immediately!' the Queen says imperiously.

The ladies run around obeying their mistress's constant instructions but nothing will soothe the Queen. All the time they attend her – removing her velvet kirtle, satin skirt, silk embroidered shirt and sleeves, boned bodice, linen petticoat and heavy Spanish farthingale – the Queen rants and raves about the shortcomings of the Duke of Anjou.

'Diminutive with a twist in his eye and his liking for the ladies is well known,' she seethes. 'My statesmen will not fob ME off with husbands who displease me. I will not make a marriage to suit Walsingham. My mother lost her head to a man – God's Wounds, I will keep mine!'

Thus shouting and swearing, Elizabeth leaves the Privy Chamber with Lady Blanche running after her with a riding whip and gloves. But when the Queen sees her handsome 'Master of the Horse' waiting to greet her she smiles in delight and her blue eyes sparkle with excitement.

'Come my lord, help me chase off my evil mood!' she laughs and, slipping her arm through Dudley's, she quits the Palace of Whitehall with a light-hearted skip in her step.

'Phew!' gasps Dido as she slumps into the nearest chair. 'Praise God she's gone!'

''Tis ever so,' muses Thomasina. 'The Queen will go so

far with her statesmen arranging a marriage, but at the point of signing she balks like a horse at a jump set too high.'

'She was in a devilish temper throughout her dealings with Philip of Spain,' Bess Throckmorton recalls. 'First she would have him, then mayhap and finally nay!'

'He dealt a hard bargain for her hand,' Thomasina answers in the Queen's defence. 'He would have claimed her country, her people and her land. She would have handed over her power to him.'

'Elizabeth will *never* share England and her throne with anybody,' Dido says quietly.

Bess and Thomasina whirl round on her and ask in joint amazement, 'How know you this?'

Deciding not to get too complicated Dido simply says, 'She's not the marrying kind!'

With the Queen out of the way, Bess Throckmorton slips away to visit Sir Walter Raleigh in the Tower of London.

'I have made him sweetmeats to sweeten his mood,' she says with a saucy wink. 'I've also employed myself in telling the Queen what a good, kind, loyal servant Sir Walter is. I see her mood doth shift when she is away from Walsingham's slanderous wagging tongue. I vouchsafe I will have my Walter out of the Tower and back in favour very soon.'

Thomasina shakes her head and smiles at Bess'

cunning plan. 'You are besotted by the seafarer and he doth use you like a moppet!'

Bess shrugs her shoulders and giggles. 'I like him well and would not see him waste away in the Tower,' she says as she hurries off with sweetmeats to tempt his love.

When the Queen returns she is in a calmer mood, but anxious to be off again.

'Bring my travelling clothes, Dorothea,' she commands. Dido's heart sinks into her soft leather boots. Surely they can't be moving palace *again*? Thomasina asks the questions which Dido hasn't the courage to voice.

'Where do you journey, Your Majesty?'

'To visit my Conjuror at Mortlake,' says the Queen with a quick smile. 'Lord Dudley has advised me to seek the good doctor's advice. My Conjuror has never failed me nor put his needs above my own, like others in my court!' she adds in a loud voice as if she hopes that those who might be spying on her will overhear her words. 'Sir Francis Walsingham will accompany me, for I am determined to rid his mind of all prejudice concerning Doctor Dee. You shall also accompany me, Thomasina, for I know you have a fondness for the good doctor and his books,' the Queen adds graciously.

Seeing Dido's beseeching eyes, the little maid drops a curtsey and says most demurely.

'Your Majesty, may we take Lady Dorothea with us to

Mortlake … she hath a great yearning to see the doctor's library.'

The Queen looks studiously at her new Lady of the Bedchamber.

'Ay, you may come, child. Now dress me quickly!'

~ 11 ~
A ROYAL VISIT

With Doctor Dee in his library, fawning on his Skryer's every word, Joshua stays well out of his way and plays with the doctor's children in the warm sunny garden.

Arthur, the eldest child, wants to play football with a pig's bladder filled with air. The pig's bladder ball is not up to Premier League standards, but Joshua is glad to run about after Arthur, who squeals with delight every time Joshua dribbles the ball around him. Katherine asks Joshua to play 'Foxes and Chickens', which Joshua's not familiar with. But when she shows him the game he realises it's just 'Catch' or 'Tag', which he played endlessly when he was a little kid.

Joshua feels better out in the sunshine, less oppressed and anxious than he is indoors, where he's seen too many changes come over Doctor Dee since the Skryer's unfortunate arrival. He's worried for his own well-being too. If Lumaluce did indeed send Joshua to Doctor Dee to be protected from Leirtod, then the good doctor's not doing a great job of it! It would have been a great choice had not Edward Kelley turned up. Unfortunately, the doctor's obsession to learn the Language of God and find the Philosopher's Stone has driven Joshua's needs right out of his head. Joshua feels like he's more open to evil in Mortlake with the Skryer calling up angels and waking the dead than he would be in Shakespeare's Chippy on the South Bank. Joshua decides that when he has a private moment alone with the doctor he may remind Dee of his promise and hopefully revive his interest in educating his protégé.

Feeling calmer and clearer, Joshua follows the children into the kitchen, where Arthur promises to find them fresh milk and honey cakes – but Joshua gets no further than the hall. He collides full on with Mistress Dee in the oak-panelled corridor that leads to the library. She's white of face and running as if the Devil himself were at her heels. When she sees Joshua, she grabs hold of him like a lifeline.

'A royal messenger has just arrived,' she says in a voice thick with dread. 'The Queen in the company of Sir Francis Walsingham is in Wimbledon and on her way to consult with my husband!'

Joshua immediately understands her fear.

'What about Edward Kelley?' he whispers.

'We must get him away!' Mistress Dee cries. 'Come help me warn my husband, for he will not heed a word I say these days,' she adds as she rushes into the library.

They find Doctor Dee and Kelley poring over ancient charts engraved on yellowed parchment that is so old it's crumbled at the edges. Mistress Dee throws herself hysterically upon Doctor Dee, who looks deeply irritated by her intrusion.

'Get thee hence, wife. I have important work to do with Master Kelley,' he snaps.

Joshua speaks on her behalf.

'A messenger arrived from the Queen, sir – she is in Wimbledon and bids you be ready to welcome her.'

The doctor hardly bats an eyelid.

'Fi! This is not uncommon, Joshua. Her Majesty often seeks me out when she is impatient to know the good omens in her horoscope.'

'She travels with Sir Francis Walsingham,' Joshua adds.

Mistress Dee's eyes turn on Kelley.

'The royal messenger was one of Walsingham's men,' she tells him.

'Was he fat and red-headed?' Joshua asks quickly.

'Aye,' the mistress replies.

Joshua turns to Doctor Dee and says, ''Twas the spy Ingram Frizar, sir.'

'He questioned me close as to the whereabouts of a certain Master Kelley,' Mistress Dee continues.

'Did you tell him anything?' Dee asks.

Mistress Dee shakes her head vigorously.

'Wouldst thou take me for a simpleton, sir?' she replies. 'We would be burned at the stake if Walsingham knew we were harbouring a *runaway priest*.' She says the last two words in barely a whisper and waits for her husband's reaction, which is instant. The blood drains from his face and he whirls on Kelley who drops to his knees.

'*You* are a *priest*?' Dee whispers incredulously.

With his monk-like hood around his shoulders revealing the hole where his ear should be, Kelley grasps the hem of Doctor Dee's red velvet gown.

'Save me, lord, save me!' he implores.

Mistress Dee tugs at her husband's sleeve.

'You cannot save him!' she cries in a frenzy of fear. 'It is too late.'

Dee pushes her aside.

'I *can* save him,' he says. 'I can hide him in the priest hole.'

'Holy Mother of God – NO!' wails Mistress Dee.

Dee stops in his tracks and glares at her.

'Wife! You will control your tongue!' he shouts as he glares at her. 'Listen carefully to what I have to say,' he adds in an icy-cold voice. 'When the Queen and Sir Francis Walsingham arrive, bring them swiftly into my library. When you do so, immediately stand upon the spot which I shall vacate. Do you understand me, wife?'

'You would have me stand over the priest hole?' she mutters mutinously.

He nods curtly.

'Do *exactly* as I say.'

Mistress Dee runs to check the whereabouts of her children, then stands by her front door in readiness for the royal arrival.

Doctor Dee tells Joshua to remain in the library, where

the doctor quickly counts the flagstones running across the floor.

'One, two, three, four, five, six, seven – that one there! Help me lift it.'

Gasping and spluttering, the three of them strain to raise the stone which once upright reveals a narrow dark space below. Dee pushes Kelley towards the priest hole, but he draws back in fear.

'How will I breathe down there?' he asks.

'It has been used before and is well ventilated,' Dee assures him.

Hearing the clattering of approaching feet in the oak-panelled corridor and the warning voice of Mistress Dee speaking extra loudly, Kelley leaps into the hole, which Dee and Joshua immediately cover by lowering the flagstone back into place. Doctor Dee then stands on the stone, arranging his flowing red velvet gown about it.

'Read to me,' he whispers to Joshua, who grabs the first book to hand and reads out loud.

'The Northwest Passage is the swiftest route to the New World, which hath yielded up great treasures of rich iron ores ...'

Joshua stops as the Queen of England walks into the room with Sir Francis Walsingham. As Doctor Dee executes an elaborate bow to the royal personage, Joshua suppresses a gasp of delight as he spies Dido and Thomasina waiting in attendance on the Queen. Dido presses a warning finger to her lips and Joshua immediately controls his facial expression so that no one might guess his joy at the sight of his friend.

Wearing a magnificent gown of red and gold brocaded velvet encrusted with tiny seed pearls, Queen Elizabeth approaches Doctor Dee, holding out a bejewelled hand for him to kiss.

'My Conjuror!' she cries playfully. 'I missed you sorely at the Palace of Whitehall.'

As the doctor moves towards the Queen, Mistress Dee neatly steps onto the flagstone over the priest hole. Her wide skirts completely cover it and any telltale signs that might suggest it has recently been moved.

Bowing low before the Queen, Doctor Dee replies with practised humility, 'A thousand pardons, Ma'am. My studies kept me from your illustrious presence.'

The Queen turns to Sir Francis, whose dark beady eyes are staring with deep intensity at Doctor Dee.

'Would you not say, good Secretary of State, that my Astrologer tarries too long at Mortlake?'

'He that tarries too long without your permission risks your displeasure, Ma'am. The Queen's desires are omnipotent to all who serve her,' he adds with an oily smile.

Dee is no fool and answers back quickwittedly, 'But sir, I am about the Queen's business.' He points to the navigational charts on the table, quickly laid over the ancient ones he was poring over only half an hour since with the Skryer. 'The Queen instructed me to chart a passage for Master Martin Frobisher's expedition to the New World.'

Any resentment in the Queen's face is replaced by a smile of delight.

'Master Frobisher has my blessings on his venture,' she says enthusiastically. 'He sails in June and our hopes are high that he will return with a cargo of gold.'

Doctor Dee does not mention his disapproval of such an early sailing date nor his anxiety about the small, ill-equipped vessels Frobisher will set sail in. Instead he smiles and bows again.

'The navigational chart is ready for Master Frobisher's collection, Ma'am.'

The Queen immediately turns the tables on Walsingham.

'See, Secretary of State!' she says triumphantly. 'My Conjuror has been working on my behest, thereby bringing much-needed treasure into our empty state coffers.'

She glares at Walsingham with her small blue eyes. 'It appears that the good doctor in Mortlake may provide me with more gold than *you* and my Statesmen in the Privy Council at the Palace of Whitehall!'

The Secretary of State bows humbly, but Joshua doesn't miss the flash of anger in his brooding dark eyes. Turning her back on Walsingham, the Queen beams at Dee.

'You have plotted a safe route through the treacherous Northwest Passage for my seafarers?' she enquires solicitously.

'Aye, lady,' he assures her. 'I have also consulted the records of Christopher Columbus' journey to the New

World. If a Spaniard can succeed,' he jokes, 'a brave English nobleman will *surely* achieve greater success!'

The Queen enjoys his quip and laughs as she nods her head in agreement with him.

'The court is in the grip of gold fever – I hope for a high return from Master Frobisher.'

Elizabeth's eyes suddenly settle on Joshua, who shifts and bows like a clumsy clown.

'Who have we here, Doctor Dee?'

'My young apprentice, Master Chai,' the doctor replies. 'He reads well, Ma'am.'

'I too have a young reader,' says Elizabeth as she beckons Dido forwards. 'Lady Dorothea, my new Lady of the Bedchamber. A sweet maid most gifted in languages, science and poetry. Doth she not remind you, sir, of myself when I was a chit of a girl, a young princess at Hatfield House?'

The Queen eyes Doctor Dee as she clearly waits for an appropriate compliment from him.

'She does indeed bear a likeness to Your Majesty as a girl ... though not as wondrous fair as thee, Ma'am,' he adds with a charming smile.

Suitably flattered, the Queen continues on an upbeat note.

''Tis a joy that so many young men and women can read and write. 'Twas not so in the reign of my sister Mary, nor my father King Henry,' Elizabeth adds as a pointed reminder of her liberal reign.

'You are as generous as you are enlightened, Your Majesty,' says Walsingham as he bows low before her.

The Queen accepts his praise with casual indifference and seats herself at Doctor Dee's desk.

'My Secretary of State would speak with you, Doctor Dee.' She turns to Walsingham. 'Tell the good doctor what your Agents Provocateur Ingram Frizar hath uncovered, Councillor.'

Walsingham wrinkles his brow.

'Forgive me, Your Majesty, my clerks can hardly be described as *Agents Provocateurs*.'

'What else would you have me call them – spies and you the Master Spy?'

Suddenly the Queen spots Mistress Dee still standing. 'Pray madam, be seated?' she says graciously.

Doctor Dee's eyebrows shoot up in alarm, but Mistress Dee remains composed.

'I thank you, Ma'am, but I prefer to stand in the presence of Your Majesty,' she answers modestly.

The Queen waves a hand at Walsingham.

'Proceed!'

The Councillor's dark calculating eyes settle on the doctor.

'I am searching for a man who presently goes under the name of Edward Kelley.' He pauses to see if Dee reacts, which he doesn't. Joshua does – his heart starts to bang like a drum! 'He uses several names,' Walsingham continues. 'Zoppo Magnus, Saul Talbot and Father Francis, a

Catholic priest from the parish of Preston, Lancashire. My informer tells me that a Skrying agent brought Edward Kelley to Mortlake several days ago.'

Doctor Dee shows a flash of temper.

'You have had your spies at Mortlake, sir?' he snaps.

'Edward Kelley has been under my surveillance,' Walsingham replies smoothly.

Joshua holds his breath and wonders how the doctor is going to wriggle out of this very tight spot …

'Kelley was sent to me by Sir Walter Raleigh,' Doctor Dee replies evenly. 'He has an interest in ancient manuscripts and Raleigh suggested he should examine my rare text on the Hebrew alphabet, which I bought in Louvain in my student days.'

'Is that *all* he did?' Walsingham asks. 'Did he not skry for you, doctor?'

The doctor does not answer directly, but cleverly prevaricates.

'I am a scientist, sir,' he answers with dignity.

'You study Archemastry,' says Walsingham as if it were an offence.

'Yes. I use crystals for stargazing, but that does not mean I am a caller-up of devils,' Dee replies firmly.

'He is my Court Astrologer,' the Queen sharply reminds Walsingham. 'Of course he uses crystals and mysterious instruments to measure the stars and the movements of the planets; how else could he execute his scientific studies, sir?'

Her impatient words make Walsingham switch tack. He drops the skrying issue but picks up on the Catholic one.

'Did Kelley say mass here?' he enquires.

'He is no priest,' Dee answers forcefully.

'He is an ordained priest,' Walsingham assures the doctor. 'Did anybody in your household know of Kelley's true profession?'

Mistress Dee sways as if she might faint with fear, but Doctor Dee remains calm and coherent.

'Nobody in my household knew of his profession.' He pauses and turns to Her Majesty.

'Was Sir Walter Raleigh privy to this information, Ma'am?' he enquires.

Clever Doctor Dee knows that Raleigh, though presently in disfavour, is one of the Queen's men who she would fiercely defend against any treasonable accusations.

'Forsooth, Sir Walter would not harbour a Catholic priest on the run – and neither would good *Doctor Dee*!' the Queen exclaims as she rises impatiently from the chair. 'Is Master Kelley gone hence?' she asks Dee sharply.

'Long gone,' he assures her.

Satisfied with his answers, the Queen addresses Walsingham.

'I am satisfied that my Conjuror speaks the truth, as well you should be, Councillor.'

Walsingham bows low before her.

'Your Majesty,' he replies obsequiously.

The Queen, having concluded one subject, moves on to the next.

'We shortly travel to Nonsuch Palace for some pleasing country air,' she announces. 'I expect you to join me there immediately, Court Astrologer,' she says in a voice that brooks no disagreement. 'I have need of your guidance concerning Frobisher's venture and other important matters of state.'

Doctor Dee and Lord Walsingham accompany the Queen to the royal carriage, where Lady Blanche Parry sits waiting for Her Majesty. Joshua, Thomasina and Dido trail in their wake, eager to snatch a moment alone. Doctor Dee helps the Queen into the wagon then bends low to kiss the extended royal hand.

'Remember Conjuror, I have urgent need of you,' says Elizabeth. 'Farewell!'

The wagon, heavily canopied with the red and gold royal coat of arms, rolls off flanked by mounted guards. When the Queen is barely out of earshot, Walsingham turns to Dee, his face set hard with dislike.

'I shall visit Mortlake more often, good doctor,' he says in a voice heavy with sarcasm. 'The Queen underestimates you … there is great knowledge in your library that I desire to uncover,' he adds as he mounts his horse, which Joshua notices is held by the red-headed Ingram Frizar.

Walsingham impatiently waves his hand towards the

second carriage, wherein Dido and Thomasina are seated.

'Move along!' he snaps irritably.

As Joshua closes the door on the two girls, Dido snatches his hand and whispers, 'Have you seen Leirtod?'

Joshua nods and whispers in reply, 'He found me here after the Skryer summoned him up.'

'You *must* come to Nonsuch Palace with Doctor Dee,' Dido says urgently. 'We have to stay together, Joshua!'

'I will – I *promise*,' he whispers as the wagon rolls off.

Doctor Dee and Joshua stand watching the royal procession rumble down the narrow lane.

'Ah, the Queen knows no peace and is forever restless in her movements,' says Doctor Dee with a weary sigh. 'I blame her father. He regularly sent her from his sight in order to appease his many wives. 'Twas better so … at least Elizabeth kept her head and did not lose it like her mother before her. Come, Chai,' says the doctor as he starts to walk quickly back to the house. 'We must release Master Kelley and prepare ourselves for *another* journey.'

Joshua wonders if Dee will be mad enough to take the Skryer with him to Nonsuch Palace.

'What will you do with Edward Kelley?' he asks nervously.

'He must go into hiding,' the doctor replies. 'But I will not lose sight of him. When the Master Spy's eyes are not upon me, I will seek out my Skryer and together we *will* search out the Philosopher's Stone – this I promise on the Cross of Christ!'

Joshua hurries along behind the doctor, eager to say something on his own behalf.

'I look forward to spending time alone with you ... I need knowledge if I am to fend off Leirtod,' he adds as a reminder. 'I would be grateful for all that you can impart to me, sir,' he finishes humbly.

'I have not forgotten my promise to you, Chai,' says the doctor softly. 'With the Skryer gone, I shall turn all my attentions to you, that I promise.'

— 12 —
DEPARTURES

Dido has never felt so weary in all her life. The joy of seeing Joshua, followed by the immediate stress of leaving him, combined with the journey back to the Palace of Whitehall in a wooden wagon that bounced and rolled over every rut, leaves her bruised and exhausted. She would give her gold and turquoise studded tiara for a long soak in a hot bath followed by a night on the sofa watching videos and eating pizza! But Elizabeth I has other plans, which are immediately put into execution via the Mistress of the Robes, Lady Blanche Parry. Dido is astonished to see Lady Blanche step out of the royal carriage alone.

'The Queen has gone on ahead to Nonsuch Palace,' Lady Blanche announces.

'Where are Sir Francis Walsingham and Master Frizar?' Thomasina enquires nervously.

'They were detained by urgent business in Wimbledon,' Lady Blanche replies. 'Now make haste – we must pack,' she adds in a fidgety voice.

'Can't we go *tomorrow*, my lady?' Dido implores.

'Lady Dorothea, it will take what remains of the day and most of the night in order to depart on the morrow,' snaps Lady Blanche irritably.

Dido feels mutinous. Why doesn't *anybody* in the royal court apply a bit of logic to all their comings and goings? It's all right for the Queen – she just sends a messenger on ahead to inform the royal household she's visiting to make ready for her. The retinue of servants left behind are responsible for the transportation of all her goods and chattels, which Dido knows from experience is similar to Hannibal moving his elephants over the Swiss Alps! She bobs a polite curtsey and says, 'I beg pardon, Ma'am … but do we have to take many dresses to Nonsuch? I mean, will Her Majesty wear five hundred?'

'You are fortunate that we do not transport a *thousand*!' Lady Blanche retorts.

'But if we are in the country the Queen will not need all of her heavy brocaded state dresses?' Dido insists.

'I know not what Her Majesty will need at Nonsuch, nor who she will entertain … There is talk that the Duke of Anjou himself may visit. Therefore we must take the entire royal wardrobe – so let us not waste time discussing the matter further,' says Lady Blanche with a sharp nod of her head.

So back in the Privy Chambers Dido, Bess Throckmorton and Thomasina are once more up to their knees in a sea of clothes. Lucky Lady Mary Sydney, who is clearly the Mistress of the Robes' favourite maid, has been swept away to help with the packing of the royal jewellery.

'It's ridiculous to keep dragging these stupid far-thingales all over England!' Dido rages as she yet again presses the awkward rope-wrapped Spanish farthingales into the clothes chests. 'Can't the Queen manage with one or two, then we could leave the other half dozen behind?'

Thomasina laughs at Dido's cross face.

'You are so angry, Dorothea,' she chides gently.

Dido, who's had enough of being a royal handmaiden, replies, 'I'd put a gold sovereign on the Queen leaving for Greenwich Palace just as we stagger into Nonsuch!'

'You are witty, Dorothea,' laughs Thomasina. 'Take comfort ... You will see Master Chai at Nonsuch and I will have time to spend in discussion with Doctor Dee.'

Dido nods her head. She's looking forward to being with Joshua but she still hasn't finished her list of grumbles.

'*And* we've missed out on the entertainment,' she adds resentfully.

'Ay, our hasty departure prevents the Chamberlain's Men from entertaining us here at Whitehall,' Thomasina agrees.

'Oh, fiddle!' giggles Bess, who even in the midst of packing a clothes chest is as happy as a skylark on a summer's day. 'The Chamberlain's Men can travel to Nonsuch and entertain us there. They say the plague has returned to the South Bank, so the playhouses will surely close.'

'Master Shakespeare will be glad to quit the city for the country if the plague is rampant,' Thomasina says.

'But Shakespeare and the Chamberlain's men could

carry the infection with them to Nonsuch Palace!' Dido cries out in alarm.

'Nay, the plague thrives only near filthy water and poor housing. The South Bank is an open sewer fit only for the habitation of pigs,' Thomasina replies.

Dido forbears to mention that she *likes* living on the South Bank – and she's not a pig! She also can't believe that somebody as bright as Thomasina doesn't understand that infection can be spread by people travelling about the country – it could even be carried on the air. Dido's thoughts are distracted by Bess, who is full of girlish laughter.

'What change has come over you, lady … ?' Thomasina enquires. 'Yesterday you were bewailing Sir Walter Raleigh's imprisonment, yet today you are smiles and dimples.'

'A *joyful* change has come over me!' Bess exclaims. 'Sir Walter Raleigh is released from the Tower and will travel down to Nonsuch to entertain the Queen.' Bess claps her hands with excitement and skips around the royal four-poster bed.

'Oh! I shall see my handsome lord soon … and he hath promised me a kiss for every sweetmeat I gave him in his dreary prison cell.'

Thomasina shakes her head.

'Lady, you have lost your wits!' she exclaims. 'He will be reading his love poems to our sovereign lady and you would be best advised to shun his presence.'

'Sir Walter may read his love poems to her, but they are

intended for me,' Bess says with undisguised delight. 'He thought of me during his sojourn in the Tower and crafted gentle words for my delight.'

Even Dido, with all of her twenty-first-century liberal thoughts, is startled by Bess' impetuosity. To flirt with one of the Queen's admirers can only lead to disaster.

'Have a care, Bess. The Queen is a jealous woman,' says Dido.

'Oh, I am sick of walking in the shadows – he loves me!' Bess says with passion burning in her voice.

'He may well love you, but his first loyalty is to the Queen – and she will watch his movements like a cat watches a mouse,' Thomasina warns.

'As will Walsingham,' Dido adds. 'His spies will shadow Raleigh – if he should put a foot wrong he'll be back in the Tower and forsooth you may well be with him, Bess!'

The ladies of the Bedchamber cease their gossiping as Lady Blanche hurries into the Privy Chamber with a pile of curled red wigs, which she drops onto the Queen's bed. Dido shudders at the sight of them.

'Lady Dorothea, if you should see one tick or flea crawling amongst Her Majesty's hair pieces I pray you do not drop them into the river, for the Queen has need of them at Nonsuch Palace!'

At Mortlake, Mistress Dee is almost swooning with fear.

'Husband!' she cries, as she falls at his feet and grips his red velvet gown in her hands. 'Do not leave Edward Kelley at Mortlake during your stay at Nonsuch Palace. He will eat us out of house and home and steal all the books from your library!'

Doctor Dee takes his wife's trembling hands in his.

'Jane, fret not. I will see Kelley safely gone before I depart,' he says tenderly.

'Oh, John!' she gasps. 'I fear for you.'

The doctor smiles confidently.

'I shall visit the Queen, advise her well and return home to Mortlake with no harm done,' he assures her.

'How long will you be gone, sir?' Mistress Dee enquires.

Dee lifts his shoulders and gives an eloquent shrug.

'The Queen is much troubled on the subject of the forthcoming match with the Duke of Anjou. Having abandoned Prince Philip of Spain as a consort, and much upset her Privy Council in the doing, she is keen to avoid disappointing them further.'

'Then she should marry the Frenchman and bring the business to a close,' replies Mistress Dee briskly. 'She spins out a yarn for I believe she hath not the slightest intention of marrying any man – apart from Dudley, who pleaseth not her Statesmen.'

'He pleaseth not me!' Dee replies forcefully. 'His star chart reads well for the present, but it ends in a dark and violent death.'

'You must inform the Queen!' insists his wife.

Doctor Dee shakes his head.

'I think not, lady. The Queen desires to hear only the good that lies ahead. Now if you will excuse us,' says Doctor Dee as he heads for the door, 'Master Chai and I must release Edward Kelley from the priest hole!'

When they lift the flagstone, they find Kelley white faced and shaking with terror.

'Thanks be to God!' he exclaims as he literally leaps out of the priest hole. 'I thought I would be buried alive down there.'

'I would not see you dead, Edward,' says Dee as he looks the Skryer firmly in the eye. 'Have you forgot the mysteries we have yet to unfold together … ?'

Kelley makes an impatient movement – he's clearly no longer preoccupied with pleasing his benefactor.

'I cannot remain here,' he says abruptly.

Seeing Kelley on the verge of flight, Dee catches hold of his arm.

'There are things left unsaid,' he says with quiet intensity. 'Is it true that you are a consecrated priest?'

Kelley nods.

'I was a Catholic priest, but as I have no church or parish to practise in or bishop to lead me I make my way by other means.'

'You put my household at risk,' Dee says gravely.

'Ah, but *you* wanted something from me, doctor,'

Kelley answers slyly. 'And I believe I gave you more than you dreamed of.'

Doctor Dee's voice falters as he questions Kelley further.

'I *need* to trust you. Tell me the truth – have you joined the Infernal Regiment?'

Kelley snatches his arm away from the doctor's grip.

'Nay, sir! I have not bartered with Satan,' he retorts angrily. 'Enough of your questions – I must be gone.'

'You'll need money,' says Dee as he reaches into a casket on the table and draws out a leather pouch. 'Use this to hide yourself until it is safe for us to meet again. When it is safe, I will find you through your Skrying agent.'

Kelley's manner changes as he feels the weight of the pouch in his hand.

'I assure you, sir, we *will* search out the Philosopher's Stone and renew our acquaintance with the archangels,' he promises as he stoops to kiss the doctor's hand.

Doctor Dee pats Kelley warmly on the back.

'I pray that day may come soon. Now hasten to your room and collect your belongings, then meet me in my Laboratory.'

'For what purpose, sir?' Kelley asks.

'You cannot leave by the front door,' Dee tells him. 'Walsingham will not have left my house unwatched. I wager one of his spies lurks outside recording my every movement. The priest hole connects to an underground tunnel that will bring you out on the other side of Mortlake church.' He smiles as he adds, 'Didn't I tell you that it was well ventilated?'

Doctor Dee and Joshua hurry into the Laboratory where the chemical stills continue to bubble over more rich concoctions of eggshells and horse dung! Doctor Dee takes up a candle and goes along the Laboratory wall, pressing his hand against the wooden panels.

'Here it is,' he says as he leans his weight against a section of panelling that swings back to reveal several steps leading down into a tunnel.

Joshua shivers as the dank air wafts out and hits him.

'How long is it since you last used the tunnel?'

'By answering that question I would be telling you something, Master Chai, that I would rather you were not privy to,' Doctor Dee replies enigmatically.

Joshua instinctively knows from his reply that the doctor has harboured Catholic priests on the run before. The sound of Kelley's approaching footsteps stops Joshua from asking any more incriminating questions.

'I'll lead the way,' says Doctor Dee. 'Chai, bring up the rear – and be sure to close the door behind you.'

The doctor's candle may well light his path but Joshua, stuck behind Kelley's bulky body, can't see a thing. Spiders' webs brush against his face and cling to his nose, making him sneeze.

'Ssshh!' hisses Dee. 'We are approaching the church crypt!'

Joshua's skin creeps. Aren't crypts the places where bodies are interred? Is he brushing against long-buried bones? Tibias and fibulas, femurs, sternums and skulls! Just as Joshua's imagination is about to send him into a frenzied panic attack, the doctor's candle throws a flickering light on a narrow slit in a thick, stone wall. Doctor Dee hitches up his red velvet gown and climbs through the gap, followed by Kelley, who has trouble getting his portly belly and ample bottom through the space. Skinny Joshua leaps through, but his relief at being out of the spooky tunnel is marred by the sight of the crypt, which he literally falls into.

'UGH!' he exclaims as the spluttering candlelight reveals a pile of bones.

Long bones, thin bones, backbones, hip bones, knee bones, ankle bones, even toe and finger bones have all been shovelled into a corner. Intact skeletons recline on stone benches: some with their leg bones dangling down, giving the impression that the skeleton is about to get up and walk out of the crypt! There are tombs too, with elaborate carvings of white marble knights and ladies laid out in eternal rest. Their hands are folded in silent prayer, and their feet rest on carved marble dogs, small company for them in the afterworld.

On tiptoe, Doctor Dee creeps towards a flight of stone steps which lead into a beautiful little church with tall fluted columns.

'Don't walk down the nave – you may be seen,' the doctor tells Joshua, who's wandered off to stare at a richly coloured wall painting of St Christopher carrying the child Jesus across a raging river.

Hugging the shadows, they creep along the side aisles and come to a small door in the north wall, which the doctor pushes open.

'Listen well, Master Kelley,' Doctor Dee whispers as he points to a small oak wood just beyond the boundaries of the church wall. 'Yonder wood will give you cover until nightfall. I've studied my meteorological charts and can assure you it will be a clear dry night. Once dusk falls, follow the cart track which leads to Cheam; from there you can easily make your way to London.'

Kelley, who now has the look of a hunted animal, nods briefly and without a farewell he races out of the church and disappears into the thick green wood. Doctor Dee stares into the empty space long after the Skryer has gone.

'With Kelley go my hopes of finding the Philosopher's Stone,' he murmurs sadly.

Joshua finally asks the question that's been on his lips a hundred times. 'How do you know he's telling you the truth?'

'I don't – but no man could have devised the visions I was privy to. He is the greatest Skryer I have known, Master Chai.'

'But he's a dangerous man – a wanted man,' Joshua says earnestly.

'You are unnerved by my fixation with him, are you not, Master Chai?' the Doctor asks softly.

Joshua nods.

'He will destroy you!' he blurts out.

'So be it. In return for what Edward Kelley will give me, I would follow him to hell and sell my soul to the Devil to boot!' With a heavy sigh, Doctor Dee turns back into the church. 'Come ... we must tarry no longer.'

Keen to avoid the spooky tunnel, Joshua asks, 'Do we *have* to go back the way we came?'

'We cannot risk walking by Walsingham's spies,' Dee points out. 'They will wonder why we did not pass them in the first place. We must return by the priest hole.'

The flickering candle they left behind has blown out and they find the crypt pitched into total darkness. As they grope their way past the tombs, Joshua stumbles into the pile of bones.

'AGH!' he screams.

As he recoils in horror, he stumbles and clutches the air. He's relieved to grip hold of some fabric, which he believes is Doctor Dee's long red gown.

'Doctor ... ?' he whispers.

'Over here,' comes the muffled reply from across the crypt. Joshua's heart starts to beat like a drum. The rough fabric in his hand can't belong to the doctor, who always wears velvet – and he knows for certain that the doctor's not standing beside him! Dropping the fabric as if it were a burning ember, Joshua tries to wriggle away, but the vapour of foul breath suffocates him. He knows without a shadow of doubt that he is *beside* Leirtod!

'Doctor Dee!' he screams, but his cries are stifled by Leirtod's thick cloak, which is pushed into his open mouth.

'Aghhhh!' he gags as Leirtod presses his face into the ground littered with brittle skeleton bones.

With his mouth stuffed up, Joshua can snatch only a little breath through his nostrils. Spluttering for air, he writhes under Leirtod's groping hands, frantically trying to break free of him.

'CHAI!' Dee calls out, as he stumbles and falls in the darkness. 'Chai! Where are you?' he calls again.

Joshua can't reply. Leirtod's hands are now around his throat and his fingers are pressing hard on the boy's Adam's apple, squeezing out the last bit of air in his lungs. Spots dance before Joshua's eyes; he can feel his body going limp. He knows he will soon lose consciousness, but he's determined not to die without putting up a fight. With all his strength, he drums his feet into the ground, sending the bones beneath his heels clattering and rolling. The noise helps Doctor Dee locate him. He literally throws himself across the crypt and lands heavily on Leirtod, who crashes full length on top of Joshua. Under the weight of the two writhing men, with hardly a breath of air left to him, Joshua faints clean away.

Locked in a fight, Leirtod and Doctor Dee roll off Joshua and spring to their feet. Unable to see each other, they grasp the air until they feel hair or flesh, which they bite and punch and kick.

Joshua comes round to hear the doctor say, 'I will die before I let you revenge yourself on the boy!'

'I have long sought him – he belongs to me,' cries Leirtod.

'Lumaluce gave him to *my* protection!'

Leirtod laughs a hard mocking laugh.

'If I were to offer you a choice here and now – *the boy or the Philosopher's Stone* – I know full well you would choose the stone and abandon Lumaluce's son.'

Leirtod pauses … Joshua hears Doctor Dee's breathing suddenly go quiet. His blood runs cold as he realises the doctor is sorely tempted by Leirtod's proposal.

'Consider … a boy's life in exchange for great knowledge,' Leirtod continues in a voice rich with persuasion. 'You would have the power to turn base metal into gold … quicken dead matter into life. You could raise the dead – like God Himself!'

Suddenly realising that he might have *two* enemies instead of one, Joshua crawls away from them as quietly as he can.

'Come doctor, make your decision,' Leirtod urges softly. 'A single knife stroke will see the boy dead, then you and I can journey to Glastonbury. By daybreak you will hold the Philosopher's Stone in your hand and I will be gone.'

As Joshua crouches in the darkness, hardly daring to

breathe, he knows that Dee is on the point of saying yes.

'Please don't betray me Doctor, please, *please*,' he prays.

'And what of the Adamic language?' the doctor asks Leirtod.

'Ah, you want that *too*?'

As they haggle over the deal that will seal Joshua's fate, he panics. Leaping to his feet, he runs headlong into the darkness and stumbles into the stack of skeleton bones, which crash to the ground making the noise of a thousand ten-pin skittles going down.

'KILL HIM!' screams Leirtod.

Gagging with fear, Joshua doesn't know where to go or what to do.

'*Help me, Father*!' he cries out in anguish.

To Joshua's unspeakable joy a light appears … He blinks hard and makes out two lights, descending the steps of the crypt.

'Who goes there?'

Booted feet clatter down the steps and by the light of the candles they're carrying, Joshua makes out the shapes of Sir Francis Walsingham and his spy Ingram Frizar.

'On your feet or I'll run you through!' Walsingham roars as he waves a razor-sharp rapier before them.

As Joshua and the doctor stumble to their feet, Joshua quickly looks around for Leirtod … but he's gone. Vanished in the blink of an eye.

'YOU!' exclaims the Master Spy as he looks into the face of Doctor Dee.

'I wonder that you are surprised, sir,' the doctor replies with an ironic smile. 'This is *my* family church.'

'Why do you lurk in the dark, doctor?' Walsingham asks with a suspicious ring in his voice.

'Young Master Chai was eager to see the effigies of my noble ancestors.' Dee points towards the white marble tombs. 'Sadly my candle blew out. I am grateful to you for coming to our rescue, sir,' he finishes politely.

'We heard a great commotion – was somebody else down here?' Ingram Frizar snaps.

'It was I who caused the disturbance,' says Joshua in a voice that's squeaky with fear. 'I'm afraid of the dark, sir. I screamed when the candle blew out,' he ends feebly.

Walsingham glares contemptuously at Joshua.

'You've wasted my time, you lily-hearted wretch!' he shouts.

'Forgive me,' says Doctor Dee. 'But I was under the misapprehension that you had left Mortlake, good Secretary of State …'

'I feigned my departure,' says Walsingham. 'I know there is a priest hole under your house, Conjuror – and I *know* you are privy to its exact whereabouts.'

'I wonder that you are so sure?' Doctor Dee enquires without batting an eyelid.

'I'm sure because I have the written word of several of your neighbours who Ingram Frizar here hath tortured most brutally to discover the truth.'

Doctor Dee's dark eyes flash with anger.

'You have tortured innocent people, sir!' he exclaims.

'They gave me the information I needed.'

'They would confess to anything under duress,' Doctor Dee protests.

Walsingham pushes his face close to the doctor's.

'Tread carefully, Magician. You may be the next to have the thumbscrews on you!'

Dee doesn't flinch but boldly holds Walsingham's gaze.

'I am under the Queen's protection,' he says with icy formality.

'I *will* find the priest hole and the skryer you protect,' Walsingham whispers malevolently. 'And when I do, I will have you both publicly disembowelled.'

With that threat echoing round the stone walls, the Master Spy and his errand boy Ingram Frizar turn on their heels and storm out of the crypt.

'Check that they've gone – *really* gone,' Doctor Dee whispers.

Joshua creeps into the church, which is empty. He hurries to the side door recently used by Edward Kelley, opens it and warily peeps out. He hears the sound of clattering horses' hooves as Walsingham and Frizar gallop away from Mortlake church.

'They've gone,' he reports back to Doctor Dee, who he finds in a pew at the front of the church with his head in his hands.

'I betrayed you, Chai.'

'I know.'

'This very day I said I would protect you … teach you everything I know. Leirtod had only to offer me the Philosopher's Stone and I was lost. I am no better than a dog!' he cries as he slumps forward and weeps with remorse.

Tears prick Joshua's eyes, but he can find no words to comfort Doctor Dee. If Leirtod were to appear right now and make the same offer, Joshua knows the doctor would indeed agree to kill his protégé. His relationship with the brilliant, wonderful genius Doctor Dee is over. Yet he must remain with him, at least until they get to Nonsuch Palace, where with Dido he might be able to think of a way of escaping the terrifying court of Queen Elizabeth I.

13
NONSUCH

Joshua's last night at Mortlake is a very uncomfortable one. He cannot help but overhear the doctor and his wife arguing in their bedchamber. Their raised voices wake the children, who cry out in distress. Katherine, the youngest, weeps for what seems like hours and finally has to be taken into her mother's bed. Joshua eventually falls into a fitful sleep, where he dreams that he's a skeleton being chased by Leirtod!

They rise at dawn, eat bread and meat and bid farewell to Mistress Dee, whose pretty face is red and swollen with crying. As she waves them off, she calls after them.

'Farewell Master Chai – come back soon, husband!'

In the open wooden cart pulled by two solid cob horses and driven by a man whose clothes seem to be made of sackcloth, Joshua has a pang of sadness. He'll never again sit at the doctor's Alchemist's desk or walk around his astonishing library stuffed with ancient books and manuscripts that pre-date Alexander the Great. Joshua knows for certain that if he were to see any of Dee's books again they would be secured behind glass in the British

Museum. He will never forget the stinking chemical stills in the doctor's Laboratory bubbling with eggshells and horse dung! He'll never see the stars from the Observatory hung like an eagle's eyrie at the top of the house. Joshua sighs and casts a glance at Doctor Dee sitting beside him with his astrological charts in a leather satchel at his feet and his shewing stone securely stored in a wooden box under his seat. A few days ago Joshua feared only demons: now he fears the doctor who was his friend.

Joshua cannot believe that the open rolling grassland, loud with the song of twittering skylarks, is *Guildford*! Where are the municipal parks, the housing estates, the traffic jams and the flyovers? Thick wooded hillsides give way to fertile valleys where occasionally a farm or a small hamlet built around a river-bend might appear. Five hundred years of development, industry and a massive population explosion have claimed this rural paradise and transformed it into a tangled network of railway lines and motorways that thread themselves through an endless urban sprawl.

Lost in thought, Joshua doesn't hear Doctor Dee. The jolting cart shakes him from his reverie just in time to catch something the doctor says – 'I will have to provide Her Majesty with a number of auspicious dates for her calendar.'

Trying to pretend that he's been listening, Joshua asks why.

'She needs to know when it will be most advantageous to write to the King of Spain who, because of the Queen's continual rejection of him in marriage, is fast turning into our national enemy. I must present her with a promising date for her meeting with the Duke of Anjou, who she now favours as a husband. I must forecast the best days for planting and reaping, hawking and hunting and graver matters too. She seeks my counsel on the subject of her cousin Mary Queen of Scots, long imprisoned in Fotheringhay Castle. Should she free her? Should she execute her? Mary is a Tudor princess! Wrong advice could bring about her beheading. Hah!' Dee sighs heavily. 'It is a wearisome heavy load to carry.'

Suddenly impatient with the steady plod of the heavy cob horses, the doctor thumps the side of the cart.

'Driver!' he calls out to the man slouched in the seat with the reins dangling from his slack wrists. 'Can you go no faster? The Queen awaits me!'

After a few cracks of the whip, the horses quicken their pace to a faster rhythm which soon sends Joshua off to sleep.

When he awakes it is to an amazing vision. The vast orange sun is setting over a huge palace, firing its many towers, cupolas, spires and turrets to a dazzling burnished gold. In Joshua's half-waking, half-sleeping state he believes he may be gazing at King Arthur's Camelot.

'Where are we?' he mumbles as he rubs his eyes against the blazing light.

'Nonsuch Palace,' Doctor Dee replies.

'It's *incredible!*' murmurs Joshua.

'Elizabeth's father Henry VIII built it after his son Edward was born. He modelled it on a French chateau – it was his hunting lodge,' Dee explains.

'*Lodge!*' Joshua laughs. 'It must have at least a hundred rooms.'

'Aye … the Queen fills them with her courtiers. It's her favourite summer palace. No doubt Lord Dudley will be at her side throughout her sojourn here,' says Dee with a disapproving scowl.

'I know I haven't been around long,' Joshua says by way of an apology. 'But I've been around long enough to know that the Queen *seriously* fancies Lord Dudley. Why shouldn't she marry him – if he fancies her, of course?'

Dee vehemently shakes his head.

'Dudley would make a *disastrous* king. He is vain, arrogant, rash and has a fiery temper that will one day be his undoing – this I *have* foreseen in the stars,' the doctor concludes grimly.

They are shown to fine chambers which are hung with rich tapestries portraying hawking and hunting scenes. They have separate bedrooms, each with a four-poster bed, again hung with heavy tapestries that hardly stir in the breeze wafting in through the open window. They share a toilet, a garderobe, which empties down a chute into the stream below. Joshua is less squeamish than he was when he arrived at Mortlake. He has become accustomed to the smells that he would find distasteful and offensive in the twenty-first century. He's now familiar with the stench of rotting waste and decomposing bodies, be it animal or human. A dead body lying in the road or a horse left to rot in the streets with the flies buzzing over it smells no better or worse than a garderobe.

No sooner have they arrived in their rooms than a servant taps on their door to say that the Queen requests Doctor Dee's presence.

'I will refresh myself and attend Her Majesty immediately,' Dee tells the servant.

When he is gone Dee examines Joshua's clothes, which are not only badly fitting but ripped and filthy dirty.

'Methinks 'tis time you had a change of clothes, Master Kai. Forsooth you cannot dine in the company of the Queen in those shameful rags!'

Joshua is sent to the tailor, who kits him out in navy blue hose and a deep purple velvet doublet with slashed sleeves of silver and gold. He's given soft leather shoes that remind him of his first pair of kids' sandals, and a purple velvet cap with a swirling black feather. What most pleases Joshua is a sword in a scabbard, which hangs around his waist on a belt elaborately worked with silver studs. He proudly swaggers before Doctor Dee, who smiles at the change in his silver-haired apprentice.

'You look like a fine Tudor gentleman,' says the doctor as he wipes a damp cloth over his own face and gives his long dark beard a brisk scrub. 'I will put on my new coat and then we are ready.'

Joshua is shocked that the doctor takes so little trouble with his appearance. Shouldn't he take a bath, trim his moustache or at least clean his teeth – even if it's only with a twig and a bit of coal dust? Doctor Dee seems content to slip into his new red velvet gown, which is only different from his old red velvet gown because it is decorated with a fine fur collar.

'Her Majesty is partial to ermine since William Segar painted her portrait with an ermine resting on her skirts,' Doctor Dee says as he concludes his preparations and picks up his satchel containing his astrological charts. 'I cannot allow the Privy Council to delude themselves into thinking the Queen's Astronomer is a man without style!' he adds as he exits the room with his head set at a haughty angle.

Before they enter the Great Hall, the doctor turns to Joshua and says, 'You are aware, Master Chai, that I must devote myself entirely to Her Majesty's pleasure?'

Joshua nods. 'I understand, sir,' he replies.

'There will be entertainment,' the doctor adds. 'There

is an outbreak of bubonic plague on the South Bank, so the Master of the Revels has invited the Admiral's Men to entertain the court here at Nonsuch.'

Joshua nods impatiently. He really couldn't care less about the Admiral's Men or the violent outbreak of bubonic plague in the city. As they approach the Queen's apartments he has one overriding thought in his head – he MUST talk to Dido!

Courtiers bow like a swaying field of wheat as Doctor Dee (with Joshua at his side) makes his way through the Great Hall towards the Queen sitting on an elaborately carved gilded chair on a high dais overlooking the vast throng. Ranged around her are her Privy Councillors: Hatton, Burghley, Cecil and Walsingham. Close to the Queen's right hand sits handsome Robert Dudley, smiling and fawning on the Queen, who turns regularly towards him to pat his hand or whisper into his ear. Joshua is not surprised to see Ingram Frizar standing at a discreet distance behind Walsingham.

'You are most welcome, Court Astrologer,' says Elizabeth with obvious pleasure. 'Have you my astrological charts about your person?'

'Aye, Ma'am, indeed I have,' says Dee as he pats his leather satchel. 'They are most auspicious, Your Majesty,' he assures her. The Queen reacts with unrepressed delight.

'We are *most* eager to hear you, good Doctor Dee,' she says as she nods towards Thomasina, who comes forward with a chair for the doctor. 'Come sit beside me, wise Astrologer,' she says as she indicates to her Privy Council to back up and make way for the Doctor. 'Let me see these good signs and omens.'

As the Queen favours her beloved Astrologer with smiles and words of praise, Joshua casts about the room looking for Dido. His heart leaps with pleasure when he sees her beckoning to him from a secluded corner behind the court musicians. Resisting the urge to run, Joshua forces himself to stroll casually along the gallery, but as he nears her, his face creases into a huge grin. Dido throws caution to the wind and hugs Joshua tightly.

'You are a fine Tudor gentleman!' she exclaims, as she admires his new clothes.

Joshua ignores the compliment and draws her further into the corner.

'Dido – I've *got* to get away from Doctor Dee,' he whispers urgently.

'*Why?* What's happened?'

'Leirtod appeared at Mortlake and tempted Doctor Dee with wonderful gifts.'

'What kind of gifts ... money, gems, Spanish doubloons?' she asks mischievously.

Joshua shakes his head.

'He offered him the Philosopher's Stone.'

'I thought that was just a book!' says Dido with a smile.

'*THIS* Philosopher's Stone is real – it's buried in the

ruins of Glastonbury Abbey in Somerset! It was put there by Joseph of Arimathea,' Joshua whispers as he nervously looks around, terrified that Ingram Frizar might be lurking behind the tapestries listening to his every word. 'It turns base metal into gold … and it quickens dead matter into living tissue!'

'Wow!' she gasps. 'No wonder Doctor Dee was willing to do a deal!'

'Thanks, Dido!' he replies, but her words bring a smile to his lips. Only *she* could make him laugh in so grim a situation.

'So how come you're standing before me alive and well?' she asks.

'I was accidentally rescued by Sir Francis Walsingham and his spy Frizar.'

'UGH!' says Dido as she shudders in disgust. 'I hate them both!'

'They found Doctor Dee and me in the crypt at Mortlake. They were looking for Edward Kelley the Skryer who we'd hid in the priest hole.'

'I have seen Edward Kelley!' Dido exclaims. 'He wears a cowled hood and has a lopped-off ear.'

'Keep your voice down, Dido,' Joshua urges. 'Ingram Frizar could be close by!'

They both drop their voices to a whisper.

'We managed to smuggle Kelley out of Mortlake, but Walsingham and Frizar found us in the crypt – just as Leirtod was about to slit my throat!'

'Hah!' gasps Dido with eyes as big as saucers.

'Doctor Dee won't protect me any more,' Joshua adds gravely. 'If Leirtod were to appear again, and he will, Dee would trade me for the Philosopher's Stone in the blink of an eye.'

'But the Doctor's a good, wise man!' she protests.

'Not when faced with wealth and power,' says Joshua grimly. 'He admitted to me that he'd follow Edward Kelley to hell and back and sell his soul to boot in exchange for the Stone. I've *got* to get away from him,' he insists.

'Where will you go?' she asks.

'*Anywhere*! But I won't leave Nonsuch without you. We must stay together.'

'I can't leave!' she exclaims. 'A Lady of the Bedchamber is the property of the Queen of England. I can't go anywhere without her express permission and to disobey her is punishable with imprisonment!'

'Then we'll have to run away, Dido.'

The blood drains from her already pale face, making the freckles on her nose and cheeks even more pronounced than usual.

'HOW?' she gasps.

Joshua shrugs.

'I don't know,' he admits. 'But if I stay, I'll surely die – and you'll be stuck in Tudor England for all eternity!' he ends dramatically. They both jump as little Thomasina suddenly appears before them.

'Dorothea! I have been looking everywhere for you,'

she chides. 'The Queen requires your services at her supper table.'

Thomasina turns to Joshua and bobs a curtsey. 'It is good to see you again, Master Chai. I hope you found Doctor Dee's library at Mortlake to your liking?'

Joshua nods enthusiastically.

'Amazing!'

'Let us talk later of the delights you found therein,' says Thomasina as she takes Dido's hand and they hurry off together.

Deep in thought, Joshua wanders through the Great Hall. He stops in surprise when he comes across a large portrait of the young Princess Elizabeth. Tall and slender in embroidered brocade, with her hair flowing over her narrow shoulders like a river of red gold, she vividly resembles Dido. No wonder the Queen is so fond of her new Lady of the Bedchamber, Joshua muses. She is a constant reminder to the world of the Queen's beautiful lost youth.

Supper is served in the great banqueting hall and Joshua is ushered to a table for the less important members of the court: the pages, secretaries, librarians and seamstresses. They all eat together – and Joshua is starving! Not a crumb has passed his lips since he shared an early breakfast with Mistress Dee and her children at Mortlake. As the feast is laid out before them, Joshua's eyes grow as big as saucers. The cooks at Nonsuch must have spent *weeks* preparing this meal! A huge roasted wild boar is placed in the centre of the serving table, decorated with caramelised apricots and spiced apple. Pheasants, quails and partridges are baked in pies running with rich gravy. There are dozens of roasted wild duck and capons, cheeses as big as coffee tables and desserts to die for: fruit junkets, creamy syllabubs, and jellies and custards in elaborate moulds.

The meal takes a long time to serve and even longer to eat. Three hours later, when the court is stuffed with fine food and fine wines, Edmund Tilney, the Master of the Revels, rises to his feet and announces the evening's entertainment.

'Your Gracious Majesty ...' he begins as he bows low in the direction of the Queen at the high table, which glitters with goblets of gold and silver, '... the Admiral's Men entertain us tonight with a fine new play which will chill your soul with tales of necromancy and devil worship!' The room is hushed as the courtiers hang on the Revel Master's every word. 'A production of *Dr Faustus* written by England's greatest living playwright, Christopher Marlowe!'

As the applause thunders out, the learned librarian beside Joshua turns to him and says, 'Mister Tilney would be wise to add, the greatest living playwright *besides* Will Shakespeare of the Globe Theatre. His Chamberlain's Men will entertain us in a lighter, merrier vein on the morrow.'

Christopher Marlowe rises to his feet and bows to his rapt audience. Joshua notes that, unlike the rest of the Privy Council, especially Lord Cecil who claps most enthusiastically, Walsingham does not applaud. His face is set hard with dislike and his whole body bristles with disapproval. He looks as if he would prefer to kick Marlowe out of the palace, but the Queen is all smiles and anticipation: she clearly approves of the handsome young man with the flowing black hair and dark brooding eyes.

'When I penned my play I was fortunate in knowing that the greatest actor in London, Edward Alleyn, would play Dr Faustus,' says Kit Marlowe. At the mention of Alleyn, the courtiers break into tumultuous applause. 'Let my play unroll,' says Marlowe with undisguised arrogance in his voice. 'Gracious Lady, I present *Doctor Faustus – the man who sold his soul to the Devil!*'

— 14 —
DOCTOR FAUSTUS

The hundreds of candles are dimmed by scurrying servants and all eyes turn towards the one source of light: a tall candelabra in a bay window which is also illuminated by the last rays of the setting sun. At a desk, identical in size and design to Doctor Dee's Alchemist's desk at Mortlake, sits Doctor Faustus. A chorus off stage starts to speak:

> *For falling to a devilish exercise,*
> *And glutted more with learning's golden gifts,*
> *He surfeits upon necromancy:*
> *Nothing so sweet as magic is to him.*

A hush descends over the captive audience as they strain to hear every syllable that drops from the lips of Edward Alleyn who, as Faustus, rises from his desk and paces his study.

> *Woulds't thou make man to live eternally,*
> *Or being dead, raise him to life again?*

A shiver of fear runs down Joshua's backbone. Can Faustus be talking about the Philosopher's Stone? The very thing that turns dead matter into living tissue! Is

Doctor Faustus like Doctor Dee, obsessed with creating life?

A Good Angel enters and urges Faustus not to be tempted, but an Evil Angel assures him he can be Lord and Commander of all the elements. Faustus cries out in delight:

> *How I am glutted with conceit of this!*
> *Shall I make spirits fetch me what I please?*
> *I'll have them fly to India for gold,*
> *Ransack the oceans for orient pearls*
> *And search all corners of the new found world*
> *For pleasant fruit and princely delicacies.*

Faustus makes his deal to sell his soul to the Devil, who appears to him in the form of Mephistopheles and Beelzebub. He is granted his heart's desire: riches, beauty, knowledge … and then his final hour on earth approaches. Sweating with fear, Faustus watches the minutes tick away: sixty, forty, twenty, ten minutes. Faustus implores mercy of the God he has so recently abandoned, but Mephistopheles, in a flowing black cloak, comes to collect his soul. As the Devil holds the flickering candelabra, Joshua gasps out loud. The flame lights up not the face of the actor, but that of Leirtod. It is Joshua's demon who whispers to Doctor Faustus.

> *Now Faustus, let thine eyes with horror stare*
> *Into that vast perpetual torture house.*
> *There are Furies tossing damned souls,*

On burning forks; there, bodies boil in lead,
There are live quarters broiling on the coals,
That ne'er can die!

Joshua's legs go to water and he starts to shake in terror. Every instinct tells him to run away, but he is mesmerised by Leirtod, who acts out his evil part to perfection. Faustus trembles in Leirtod's grip, just as Joshua did in the crypt at Mortlake.

Come not, Lucifer! I'll burn my books!

Faustus cries out, but his repentance is too late. As demons drag him off to eternal torment, Leirtod faces the rapt audience and his coal-black eyes flash vengeance. He swirls his long black cloak and then all goes dark.

Gripped with stomach-churning fear, Joshua leaps to his feet and gropes his way through the audience, desperate to get out of the presence of Leirtod.

'Sit down!' yell indignant courtiers as he treads on their toes, but sitting still, waiting to be found by Leirtod, is the last thing Joshua intends to do! Gasping for breath, he rushes forward and stumbles into somebody. Fearing it's Leirtod, he flails about with his fists, but candlelight illuminating the gallery reveals that Joshua is in the grip of Doctor Dee.

'Oh, help me, sir!' Joshua cries. 'I'm so afraid!'

'I too am sore afeared, Master Chai,' the doctor answers solemnly. 'I have seen my destiny acted out by Edward Alleyn and my soul creeps with dark foreboding.'

'Leirtod was in the play!' Joshua splutters. 'He led Faustus down into Hell.'

Doctor Dee shrugs.

'Hell is his domain … mine too if I pursue my quest for the Philosopher's Stone.'

'Abandon it, sir!' Joshua cries wildly. 'Give it up and live a happy life. Do not endanger your immortal soul,' he says, as he remembers a chilling line from the play.

The Queen rises and all conversation ceases.

'Mr Marlowe, your play is sombre indeed, but a worthy piece and one which will provide us with much thought.' It's clear she admires the play but it didn't amuse her. 'We hope you will be here on the morrow to be entertained by another great playwright and his company, Master Shakespeare and the Chamberlain's Men?'

Marlowe bows low.

'Madam, I must return to London – my mother has been taken seriously ill and I must attend her immediately.'

'You will forego the pleasures of Master Shakespeare's new play?' the Queen asks. 'We hear tell it is a sweet tragedy concerning two star-crossed lovers.'

'I must away, Your Majesty. With your permission, I leave tonight.'

Joshua stares across the gallery at Dido. Their eyes lock: *Marlowe's leaving tonight*!

'Do you plan to walk back to London?' Elizabeth quips.

'No, Ma'am.' He smiles his charming smile. 'A wagon awaits me.'

The Queen extends her bejewelled hand to the playwright.

'Then Godspeed, Christopher Marlowe,' she says as he bows to kiss her hand. 'Return swiftly and entertain us further with your great intellect.'

As Marlowe flourishes a bow, Joshua eyeballs Dido: *We have to go NOW!*

'Your Majesty,' says Dido sweetly. 'Shall I escort Master Marlowe out of the palace?'

Elizabeth looks at her handmaid fondly then pats her face.

'Good Dorothea. Go, do your duty and return swiftly – I have need of you.'

Dido casts Joshua a meaningful look as she leads the playwright out of the room. Joshua knows he has to follow her, but he cannot go without warning the doctor, for the very last time.

'Remember Faustus, Doctor Dee. Please, *please* don't sell your soul and burn in hell!' he implores with tears in his eyes.

Then Joshua turns and without a goodbye he walks away from one of the most brilliant men in history.

Luckily Marlowe has to bid farewell to his company and pick up his belongings, which gives Joshua and Dido time to work out a plan.

'I'll hide in the wagon before he comes out,' says Joshua.

'And what do *I* do?' cries Dido.

Joshua thinks hard.

'Tell the driver you have to return to the Queen, then sneak back and join me in the wagon. But be quick! Marlowe might be here any minute.'

Luckily the driver's addressing a serving wench so he barely notices Dido who bobs him a curtsey before having a brief word with him. She then hurries off, pretending to go indoors, but in fact slips into the bushes and crawls back to the wagon through a very prickly beech hedge.

Joshua is in a corner of the vehicle crouched under some stinking sackcloth.

'Get under here!' he urges.

Dido scrambles up and lies beside Joshua, who feels her trembling like a leaf in the wind.

'I'm so scared,' she whispers.

'Me too,' he admits. 'But we'll be safer in London, away from the court and all the conspiracies.'

'You mean *you'll* be safer away from Doctor Dee,' Dido mutters crossly. 'But what about ME? The Queen may have me searched out and imprisoned.'

'Shshh!' he hisses, as footsteps approach.

'Come, driver!' Marlowe calls out impatiently.

They hear him climb into the wagon and slump heavily onto a wooden seat.

'God's Wounds!' he mutters fiercely under his breath. 'Let's begone.'

As the driver lumbers into his seat, Marlowe barks at him, 'If I'm not in Deptford by dawn I'll break both your arms!'

'Y-y-yes, sir!'

The driver whacks the horses' rumps with a sharp crack of the whip and the wagon rolls forward.

Terrified they might be discovered, Joshua and Dido grip hands underneath the sacking, hardly daring to breathe. The lights of Nonsuch Palace recede and before long they are in total darkness with owls hooting eerily overhead.

'How long before we change horses?' Marlowe irritably asks the driver.

'Twenty miles down the road, sir.'

'It is *vital* that I am in Deptford by dawn,' Marlowe says again. Sensing Marlowe's potential fury, the driver urges the horses on with yet another crack of his whip. As the lumbering wagon bumps and bounces over the dirt track, Marlowe dozes in his seat and, amazingly enough, so do Dido and Joshua.

When the wagon stops at an inn to change horses, they both wake to hear Marlowe yelling at the serving boy.

'Change the horses and make it sharp. I have urgent business in Deptford.'

Telling the boy he will take ale, Marlowe hurries indoors, giving the stowaways a chance to speak freely.

'Deptford?' puzzles Dido. 'He told the Queen his sick mother was in London?'

'Deptford *IS* in London,' Joshua whispers back.

'But we're in Tudor London – it could be a village in the sticks!' Dido frets.

'Something tells me that wherever we're going is nothing to do with Marlowe's sick mother,' Joshua answers grimly.

The four horses are changed and Marlowe returns to the cart, wiping ale from his lips. The fresh new horses have put a good distance between the first inn and the next, where again Marlowe descends from the cart to refresh himself with ale.

'He'll be drunk by the time we get to London,' Joshua muses.

The driver also hurries off to partake of a tankard of ale, leaving the cart briefly unattended. Dido and Joshua take the opportunity to remove the stinking sacking from their faces and cautiously peep out.

'I wonder where we are?' Dido whispers.

A voice out in the darkness answers her question.

'Does Marlowe know anybody in Guildford …?'

Joshua's body goes tense with fear. He'd know that voice anywhere – it belongs to Sir Francis Walsingham! He peers into the soupy darkness and makes out the shape of two men on horseback.

'Marlowe has spies everywhere,' the voice of Ingram Frizar replies.

WHY are the Secretary of State and his low-life spy

following Kit Marlowe? Why aren't they at Nonsuch attending the Queen?

'We'll pick up fresh mounts and follow at a safe distance,' says Walsingham.

'Shshh!' hisses Frizar. 'He comes hither!'

As Marlowe comes out of the inn, Walsingham and Frizar slip back into the shadows.

'Get a move on!' Marlowe yells at the stable lad, who's having difficulty putting one of the horses into the shafts. He then turns to the driver and asks what their next stop might be.

'Wimbledon – if the horses are fresh,' comes back the reply.

'Get me to Deptford by dawn and I'll double your money,' promises Marlowe, who's obviously pleased at the swift progress they're making.

And off they go again. When they hear the playwright's steady snores, Dido whispers in Joshua's ear, 'Shouldn't we tell Marlowe that Walsingham is following him?'

Joshua quickly shakes his head.

'No!' he whispers back. 'He might throw us out of the wagon, then we'll have to walk to London.'

'But he might be in danger.'

Joshua shrugs.

'There's not much WE can do about it.'

They both freeze as they hear horses trotting at a distance. Marlowe awakes as if a cannon has gone off. They see his outline, straining forward as he listens attentively.

'Did you hear something out there?' Marlowe asks the driver.

'I thought I 'eard 'osses,' he replies. 'But they ain't there now, sir.'

Marlowe breathes more easily and relaxes back in his seat. As the moon sails out from behind a band of dark cloud he takes papers from his pocket which crackle in his hands as he turns them over, muttering their contents as if he knows every word off by heart.

'A network of spies in Rheims uncovered English priests in training. They are most keen to return to England and spread popery across the land.' The papers crackle louder as he scrunches them into the balls of his fist. 'Damn them all!' he curses. 'There is no God – neither Catholic nor Protestant. Let the atheist be free to speak his mind and leave religion to the simpletons!'

Marlowe doesn't go back to sleep but sits tensed and moody, occasionally muttering a blasphemous oath or cursing the driver for his slowness. The first fingers of light appear as they change horses at Wimbledon.

'I'll pay good money for the swiftest horses,' shouts Marlowe as he leaps from the cart and throws a handful of coins at the stable lad. 'Change them speedily and you shall have an extra sovereign.'

Hearing Marlowe only inches away, Joshua and Dido bury themselves deeper under the sacking.

'How far to Deptford?' Marlowe asks.

'Not far, sir?' the boy answers vaguely.

'Will I be there by daylight?'

'Oh, aye. For sure, sir.'

As they trot off, Joshua listens hard for Walsingham and Frizar. He can't hear the sound of horses' hooves … are they still following them?

As they complete the last leg of the journey they hear the city waking up. Shutters are thrown open and slops emptied into the street. Some waste falls into the cart, very close to Joshua and Dido, who have the unfortunate privilege of travelling alongside it for the next half hour! Street vendors cry their wares, women scold, children cry, dogs bark; they even hear a pig grunting as it barges past their wagon. Terrified that Marlowe may see their shapes under the sacking in the dawn light, Joshua presses himself up against Dido, who flattens herself against the side of the wagon. Fortunately Marlowe isn't interested in the contents of the wagon. Joshua can see his outline impatiently scanning the area they're driving through. When the driver announces they're in Deptford, Marlowe hails the nearest passer by.

'Where's May Bull's Tavern?'

'Up yonder street, sir,' a woman answers. 'But she may be closed at this hour.'

'She won't be closed for me!' says Marlowe with an assured ring in his voice.

When they reach the tavern, Marlowe doesn't wait for the cart to stop but leaps out, quickly throwing a bag of coins at the driver.

'You promised that you'd pay me double if I got you to Deptford by dawn,' the sullen driver protests.

'You do not please me well enough to pay double,' says Marlowe with an arrogant laugh.

The driver mutters an oath that shocks even the two street-wise twenty-first-century children hiding in his wagon. Still swearing and damning Marlowe to eternal torture, he dismounts and goes to relieve himself against the side of a house. Joshua nudges Dido.

'NOW!' he hisses in her ear.

They spring from the wagon and dart into the tavern, where they immediately hide themselves under the nearest table. In their haste to escape the driver, they run headlong into further danger. They find themselves back in the company of Kit Marlowe, who's at a nearby table talking to three men.

'Here are the names of the Catholic priests training at the English Seminary in Rheims,' says Marlowe as he pushes the sheets of paper he's been carrying across the table to the obvious leader of the three men. 'They will arrive in Folkestone before the end of July and infiltrate the houses of the powerful Catholics in the north of England. You'll find Lord Strange heads the list of treacherous Catholic conspirators.'

The leader scans the list and laughs grimly.

'We must make haste and present this to Lord Cecil, who will be most pleased to be privy to such information before it falls into the hands of Sir Francis Walsingham.'

Kit Marlowe laughs in triumph as he raises his brimming tankard to his lips.

'To the Master Spy who's in the dark!' he mocks and downs the contents of the tankard in several gulps.

Before Marlowe's had time to wipe the ale from his lips, the tavern door is flung open and Walsingham strides in with Ingram Frizar. The Master Spy's eyes flash hatred as he confronts Marlowe, who jumps to his feet so quickly he upsets the table in the process.

'YOU!' Marlowe cries in disbelief.

'Not so in the dark that we could not follow you hither,' says Walsingham.

As he bears down on Marlowe, the three men back swiftly away from him.

'How doth your sick mother, sir?' sneers Frizar as he pushes Marlowe up against the wall.

'She fares badly, sir,' says Marlowe civilly.

Though cornered, he does not seem afraid: he has an insolent sneer on his face as if Frizar were a lower life form than himself.

'We have been watching you, *double agent*,' hisses Frizar as he pushes his fat red face up against Marlowe's pale elegant one.

The poet turns his head away as if the spy's breath offends him.

'I work for my sovereign Queen,' says Marlowe with dignity.

'God's Wounds!' shouts Walsingham. 'You work for who you please! Wherever there is political intrigue you are at the very heart of it, spying and counter-spying. You are already on trial for atheism, for denouncing our Lord Jesus Christ and mocking all who believe in him as simpletons.'

Marlowe responds to Walsingham as if *he* were a simpleton.

'I beg you not to bore me with your homespun Christian rantings, good Secretary of State.'

'Mock me not, sir!' says Walsingham as his eyes bore into Marlowe's. 'We know you practise witchcraft, alchemy, devil worship, skrying and live in a doubtful underworld. And now you spy on *me* – the most important man in the land – for Lord Cecil!' he roars.

'Pray, sir, where is your proof?' Marlowe asks.

'There's my proof!' Walsingham screams as he points to the sheet of paper in the man's trembling fingers. 'The document I commissioned you to undertake you hand over to Cecil's men!'

Marlowe waves a hand dismissively in the air. He seems to be enjoying goading Walsingham, whose face is contorted with fury.

'I prefer Lord Cecil. He is a true gentleman. You, sir, walk in the shadows. You plot and intrigue, you cheat and you torture. You surround yourself with a network of spies who outnumber the courtiers two to one! You ride for a fall, Secretary of State. Lord Cecil has alerted the Queen to your political intrigues – your secret service. It is only a question of time until you wake up with a rapier in your back.'

Incandescent with anger, Walsingham turns to Ingram Frizar.

'Kill him!'

Before Marlowe can move an inch, Frizar draws his dagger from its scabbard.

'NO! NO!' screams Marlowe.

The three men abandon Marlowe to his fate and take flight, dropping the paper he took so much trouble to deliver to them. Paralysed with fear under the table, Joshua and Dido watch in horror as Kit Marlowe struggles under Frizar's grip. As the spy's dagger jabs the air above Marlowe, he frantically turns his head from left to right trying to avoid the blade … but it finds its mark. Frizar pierces Marlowe just above his right eye and the blade enters his skull by two inches. In complete agony Marlowe lets out a scream so loud it chills Joshua to the soul. In blind pain he thrashes the air, then falls to the ground with blood gushing from his gaping head wound. Like a dog, he crawls on his hands and knees, then his legs give way beneath him and he sinks down into a pool of blood right in front of Joshua and Dido. Joshua covers his mouth to stop the vomit pouring out and Dido leaps to her feet screaming hysterically. With Walsingham and Frizar they watch Marlowe twitch and shudder … then he lies motion-less at their feet.

'We are well rid of him,' says Walsingham with a ruth-less smile. His gaze lands on the two terrified children who are clinging to each other expecting the same punish-ment to be meted out on them.

'Arrest them on charges of spying!' he tells Frizar, who after replacing his bloody dagger in his scabbard grabs the two children by the hair!

'Aghhh!' they scream, as much in pain as in terror.

Walsingham stoops to pick up the papers dropped on the floor, then turns to Frizar.

'I return to Nonsuch,' he tells him. 'Take the traitors to the Tower!' he adds, and, stepping over the pool of blood in which the greatest playwright in England lies, he leaves the tavern and returns to the service of his Sovereign Queen.

-15-
THE TOWER
OF LONDON

A jailer with one eye, no teeth and hands as huge as shovels literally throws Dido and Joshua into their prison cell, where the first thing they lay eyes on is a rat as big as a dog. Both of them scream in terror and hurl themselves at the prison door, which they beat until their fists ache.

'You were *wrong*, Joshua!' cries Dido as tears flow down her cheeks as pale as death. 'We were safer at court under the Queen's protection. I should never have listened to you,' she adds with an angry sob.

'We'll get out of here,' he mutters in a voice that holds no conviction.

'Few do,' a voice mocks in the gloom.

'Wh-wh-who's there?' Joshua stutters in a high, squeaky voice.

'Someone you know well, sir,' the voice replies. A shadowy form looms towards them. 'The fair maid I have not had the pleasure of meeting, but you, Master Chai, I have spent many an hour with you—'

Joshua simply can't believe his eyes. Standing in front of him is Doctor Dee's Skryer.

'Edward Kelley!' he gasps.

'Aye, but hush your voice. I go under another name in here.' He turns to Dido, who instinctively hides behind Joshua's back. 'And your lady, sir?'

'D-D—' Joshua hesitates. Should he call her by her Tudor name or her real name? 'Dorothea,' he answers quickly.

'Come, maid, be not shy,' says the Skryer softly.

Dido looks out at him from behind Joshua.

'You are beautiful indeed,' says Kelley as his eyes sweep over her face. 'You call to mind Princess Elizabeth when she was fair and not the painted hag that we see these days.'

Dido anxiously looks towards the cell door.

'Do not speak so, sir,' she implores. 'We could be whipped for your indiscretions.'

'What care I for a whipping when I'll be hanged for treason?' says the Skryer with a shrug of his shoulders. 'But you, Master Chai ... how come you share my prison cell?'

Too tired to stand a moment longer, Dido slumps onto a heap of dirty straw while Joshua tells Kelley of Marlowe's hideous murder.

'WALSINGHAM!' Kelley cries as Joshua concludes his grim story. ''Twas he that brought me here with a promise that Doctor Dee would shortly follow.'

'The doctor's enjoying the Queen's protection at Nonsuch Palace,' Joshua assures him.

'For that I am glad,' Kelley replies with genuine sincerity.

'What charges are you accused of?' Joshua asks.

'Forging, skrying, necromancy, devil worship and trumped-up charges of witchcraft.'

'The very charges that Walsingham accused Marlowe of before his spy stabbed him to death!' exclaims Joshua.

'The Master Spy is on a witch hunt,' Kelley replies.

Joshua nods toward Dido, who is shaking with fear on her bed of straw.

'I beg you, do not upset the maid afresh. She has seen a man die most hideously in the last hour.'

Kelley takes Joshua's arm and leads him a little away from Dido.

'After my hasty departure from Mortlake I returned to Durham House in London. Sir Walter Raleigh was indisposed in the Tower, but whilst I was there I was asked to skry for Sir Francis Bacon, Sir Francis Drake and the Earls of Leicester, Norfolk and Kent.' The scar on his cheek causes Kelley to make a crooked, twisted smile. 'If Walsingham is rounding up those who have an interest in the Black Arts he might well imprison half of Her Majesty's court before he is done!'

A sudden fury overtakes Joshua, who throws up his arms in anger.

'Is there anybody in Elizabeth's court who *isn't* interested in Devil worship?' he shouts.

'Shsh!' hisses Kelley as he claps a hand over Joshua's

mouth. 'If One-Eyed Jack the guard should hear you talk of such things he'll have the thumbscrews on you to find out more.'

Joshua feels suddenly emotionally exhausted.

'It's all such *nonsense*!' he mutters wearily. 'I come from a place where we study science in school: we have a handle on reality. You lot are *crazy*! Because you don't understand how things work you let your imaginations go mad and what do you get? *Mumbo Jumbo*! You kill, you spy, you stalk, you torture, you fantasise but you never ever *understand*. I've *had* it with you Elizabethans – absolutely *had it*!'

At the end of his tirade Joshua bursts into tears, but the relief of speaking his mind gives him great comfort. 'I just want to go home,' he whispers in a forlorn voice.

'Me too,' says Dido as she huddles up close beside her friend.

'Where is your home?' asks Kelley.

'London, but another time …' Joshua mutters vaguely.

The Skryer appears unperturbed by his strange statement.

'There was something about you at Mortlake, Master Chai … ?' he murmurs.

'I did not like you, sir!' Joshua blurts out, glad that he can finally speak the truth. 'I thought you were deluding good Doctor Dee.'

'You did not see what he saw in the shewing stone,' Kelley points out.

'How would I know what he saw in the glass?' Joshua demands. 'I who saw nothing!'

'He saw what he wanted to see,' Kelley replies.

'So you did cheat him?' Joshua asks.

'Nay, not so. I gave the doctor all that he desired. It is for the receiver to do as he so wishes with what is put into his hands,' Kelley answers quietly. 'But YOU,' he continues, 'were never revealed to me in the shewing stone. I assumed it was because you are not yet a man ...' he gazes into Joshua's silvery-grey eyes. 'There is more to you,' he concludes.

'My father is Lumaluce,' Joshua answers proudly.

'I know Lumaluce!' Kelley cries. 'He has appeared to me in the shewing stone.'

'He protects me from his enemy, Leirtod, who wants me dead,' Joshua explains.

'Forsooth, Master Chai, we are all sore plagued by demons,' says Kelley sympathetically. Seeing Dido's tear-stained face staring at him woefully in the gloom, he continues in a less morbid tone. 'I discovered great treasures in Sir Walter Raleigh's library: treasures that lift my spirits even when enclosed in so dark a place as this.'

'Pray don't speak to me of forgery. I cannot bear the thought of your other ear being lopped off for further offences,' Joshua implores.

'What I discovered is worth having *both hands* lopped off!' the Skryer says with barely suppressed excitement. 'Raleigh's library, unlike Doctor Dee's, is in great disarray.

Books and charts are strewn all over the floor,' Kelley adds disapprovingly. 'After rummaging for hours, I came across a faded, barely legible manuscript that was crumbling with age. I examined it and found it to be written in neither Hebrew, Greek, Latin nor Arabic, yet it was oddly familiar to my eyes … something I had seen before.' The Skryer grips Joshua's hand. 'And then I realised I *had* seen it before – in the shewing stone at Mortlake when Uriel revealed to Doctor Dee the Language of God!'

'*WHAT*?' Joshua cries out in astonishment.

Kelley scrambles to his feet.

'Watch the door,' he commands Dido and Joshua.

To their amazement the Skryer starts to scratch about on the floor in a corner of the cell. After much prodding and poking, he lifts a loose stone and brings out a folded crumpling piece of parchment.

'Gaze upon the words that God taught unto Adam,' Kelley says with true reverence.

'You *stole* it!' Joshua splutters.

'I stole it for Doctor Dee. It would have rotted away on Walter Raleigh's filthy floor,' says Kelley with no remorse. 'I was arrested and brought here on the charges of skrying and forgery – but *not* for stealing the Language of God!' he says with delight. 'There was something else …' he adds in a whisper.

Joshua grabs hold of Kelley's arm.

'You found the ancient scroll?' he gasps.

'Aye, Master Chai, the map of Glastonbury Abbey.'

Kelley gives his crooked twisted smile as he awaits Joshua's reaction – and he does react. Joshua leaps into the air, but quickly suppresses the cry on his lips for fear of alerting the jailer. He hunkers back down on the floor close to Kelley.

'It was tossed on the ground amidst a heap of discarded paper,' Kelley replies as he shakes his head. 'Such treasures wasted on Walter Raleigh—'

'Never mind Raleigh!' says Joshua, hardly able to control the emotion in his voice. 'What did you do?'

'I went to Glastonbury, of course.'

Joshua is so flabbergasted he can barely find the breath to complete his next sentence.

'And ...?'

'I found it!' Kelley laughs out loud in pure delight. 'I found it – exactly where the map said it would be.'

'*The Philosopher's Stone!*' says Joshua in the barest whisper.

Kelley nods and produces from under the dirty straw that litters the floor a coppery red oval stone, which he cradles in his hand. Joshua looks from the Stone to the sheets of faded parchment and mutters incredulously.

'One can quicken life, the other is the word of God given to Adam before the fall ... all that Doctor Dee desires.'

''Tis a pity that he is not here to share it with us,' Kelley replies.

'Lucky Doctor Dee not to be stuck in here!' Dido says bitterly, then she amazes Joshua by turning to Edward

Kelley and saying, 'Use the Philosopher's Stone to get us out of here!'

The Skryer shakes his head.

'It doesn't open locked doors!'

Dido's brilliant blue eyes are wide with determination.

'Mr Kelley!' she says forcefully. 'With the combined forces of the Philosopher's Stone, your skrying skills and Joshua's legendary father, there *has* to be a way out of here.'

Kelley shakes his head as if she's talking gibberish, but Joshua catches Dido's drift.

'She's right,' he tells the Skryer, who's absently tossing the precious stone up into the air. 'Summon up Lumaluce in the shewing stone.'

Kelley looks at him like he's a dunderhead.

'I haven't got a shewing stone here!'

'A shewing stone is a crystal, isn't it?' Dido asks quickly.

Kelley nods in answer.

'I've got a crystal!' she announces as she reveals a large crystal hanging from a delicate golden chain about her neck. 'The Queen gave it to me at Hampton Court.' She unhooks the chain and hands the crystal to Kelley. 'Will that suffice, Master Kelley?'

The Skryer lays the Philosopher's Stone beside the sheets of faded parchment and takes hold of Dido's crystal. Joshua and Dido wait in breathless silence as Kelley's eyes turn milky white.

'What's happening to him?' Dido whispers in alarm.

'He's going into a trance,' Joshua reassures her. 'Be still and say nothing.'

Kelley's fingers uncurl and the crystal is revealed in his grimy palm. It's not clear and sparkling any more, but pulsating with light. The crystal atoms churn then settle into an image that Joshua immediately recognises.

'*My father*!' he cries.

Lumaluce is as he was the last time Joshua saw him – dressed in a short white tunic with a sword in a scabbard at his hip and gold armour strapped about his chest. The image and the crystal re-form … Lumaluce is revealed, but this time as an angel with wings of gold. Choked with love, Joshua can barely speak. He struggles to control himself and manages to say, 'Father! We're in terrible danger from Leirtod *and* Walsingham. *Please* help us to get out of here – *please* let us go home!'

In reply, Lumaluce starts to slowly flap his wings: they beat faster and faster, creating a wind which sends the parchment sheets containing the words God gave to Adam flying up into Joshua's face. He grabs them and stuffs them under his doublet. Suddenly Kelley lets out a sharp cry and Dido's crystal falls from his hand as if it were red-hot. Before it lands on the ground it has doubled in size and glows with a metallic white heat. As it makes contact with the cell floor it implodes and a light as blinding as a laser beam blazes through their cell. Covering their eyes against the blaze, they turn away and when they turn back it is to look upon Lumaluce. Joshua rushes into his arms. Lumaluce raises his son's tear-stained face and looks into the silvery-grey eyes that are so like his own.

'Joshua, fear not.'

'B-b-but we're locked up in the Tower of London!' Joshua cries out in fear.

'Doors can be opened.'

Lumaluce turns to Dido and Kelley.

'Take Joshua's hands,' he says.

Gripping Dido's hand on his right and Kelley's on his left, Joshua stands before Lumaluce, whose great wings start to burn with light.

'Do not question, doubt or hesitate,' he tells them. '*Follow me …*'

Lumaluce leads them towards the metal door of the prison cell, before which he stands with his burning bright wings. The door turns cinder red then melts away and Lumaluce walks through it. With his father beside him, Joshua knows no fear. Smiling, he leads his companions through the open door and out the other side. Now Lumaluce's no longer in front of them – he's flying overhead! Quickening their speed, they run to keep up with him.

Lumaluce leads them through a labyrinth of echoing dark, dank stone passageways that finally emerge on a flight of steep stone steps. Slipping and sliding, they hurry down the slimy steps and walk out onto a jetty, into the clear night air. A full moon sails out from behind a band of dark cloud and Joshua realises they're on the banks of the River Thames.

'God's Blood!' Kelley cries in astonishment. 'We've come out through Traitors' Gate!'

Wreathed in smiles, he grips Joshua's hand in his.

'Master Chai, I thank you and your father for my freedom. It is sweet and unexpected indeed. But I will not tarry, sir,' he adds as he throws a wary glance over his shoulder. 'The alarm will surely sound and Walsingham's men will be after us. Farewell, Chai – I shall seek you out in my shewing stone.'

Taking to his heels, Kelley disappears into the darkness where he is swallowed up like a shadow.

Joshua doesn't run. He knows his father is close by and waits for a sign. It comes. A light flickers on the water. It grows bigger as it approaches the embankment and a boat drifts into view. Lumaluce flies over the boat, guiding it towards Joshua with the beating of his wings. Dido and Joshua leap into the boat and lie in the bottom of it with Lumaluce's wings resting over them. A great peace descends over Joshua. This is the river in which his father drowned before he was born … and this is the river that will bear him home. Joshua closes his eyes and falls asleep, breathing in rhythm to the beating of his father's heart.

EPILOGUE

Joshua wakes to the sound of the boat gently nudging land ... he hears the shrill scream of a police siren followed by the steady buzz of a helicopter hovering overhead. He doesn't want to open his eyes because he knows that when he does he will not be covered by the sweep of angel's wings, he will not hear his father's heart beating in rhythm with his own: he will, in fact, be home. Dido stirs beside him.

'Joshua!' she whispers in a confused voice. 'Where are we?'

'Listen ...' he says.

Sounds that would have been alien in Tudor England assail Dido. The continuous purr of car engines ticking over, the screech of brakes, the blast from the horn of a passing motorboat, the distant chimes of an ice cream van. Dido's eyes widen with delight.

'YEAH!' she shrieks as she leaps to her feet and sends the boat perilously rocking backwards and forwards. 'We're HOME!'

'Be careful,' he cries out. 'You'll tip the boat!'

Whooping with joy, Dido picks up the hem of her richly brocaded dress and jumps out of the boat onto the bank, where she waves joyfully at the tourists gazing down at her from the slow-turning London Eye.

'I've just met Queen Elizabeth the First!' she hollers.

'You're dressed for it, love!' a jolly tourist shouts back.

Dido turns to Joshua and holds out a hand.

'Come on,' she urges.

Joshua lingers. The boat is his last link with his father.

'JUMP!' she cries.

And Joshua jumps!

As they hurry home along the towpath everybody they pass assumes they're promoting Shakespeare's *Romeo and Juliet* presently showing at the Globe Theatre on the South Bank.

'What time's the show?'

'Is it half-price for under fives?'

'Is there wheelchair access into the theatre?'

Unable to answer any of the questions, Dido and Joshua slip down a familiar side street that brings them out by the *Golden Hind.* Dido stops dead in her tracks.

'It all began here, Joshua,' she says incredulously.

Spotting their bizarre Elizabethan costumes, an American tourist asks them if they'd pose with her on the *Golden Hind.*

'You look so cute!' she enthuses.

Thinking of his terrifying encounter with Leirtod in the bowels of the ship, Joshua refuses point blank to board the *Golden Hind.*

'Let's get rid of these clothes,' he says as the woman walks away.

As Joshua impatiently unfastens the line of hook-and-eyes that run down his doublet he feels the sheets of parchment pressed against his chest.

'The Book of Adam,' he murmurs as he opens wide his purple velvet doublet.

But it is in shreds! In passing over the centuries the precious parchment has aged four hundred years and is nothing but fragments.

'NO!' cries Dido as she falls to the ground and frantically tries to retrieve the tiny pieces.

The words God gave to Adam at the beginning of time crumble in their fingertips. A passing breeze lifts them up and blows them away on the morning tide.

'Oh, Joshua!' wails Dido as she stares at the tiny specks floating on the River Thames.

But Joshua's not listening to her. He grabs her hand and grips it so tightly she gasps in pain.

'DIDO!'

'What is it?' she cries.

'If I took the Language of God ...' he stops to take a long shuddering breath, '*WHO* has the Philosopher's Stone?'

Author's Notes

My research for this book began with Elizabeth I and her fascinating court, but at every turn I came across the character of Doctor Dee: scholar, mathematician, scientist, astrologer and dabbler in the occult, he began to intrigue me. It was he who was asked to study his astrological chart and pick an auspicious date for Elizabeth's coronation: the dawn of the new Elizabethan age. He chose 15 January 1559 and on a blustery rainy day the young queen, dressed in cloth of gold with her long auburn hair worn loose about her shoulders, stepped into the pages of history. Doctor Dee and Joshua have their own secret hieroglyphs, the Greek letters Delta, δ, and Chai, χ, which is pronounced 'Kai' and represents a cross.

I found Benjamin Woolley's book *The Queen's Conjuror* invaluable and completely riveting reading. Sir Walter Raleigh, the Privy Council and Christopher Marlowe, who was known to be a spy, were all real people who would have been at Elizabeth's court. The Skryer Edward Kelley really did skry for Raleigh's School of the Night, with which Marlowe too was involved. Marlowe died in 1593, so I have taken a few liberties with dates here and elsewhere for the purposes of the story. It isn't known exactly when Marlowe's *Doctor Faustus* was first performed, but it seems likely that it would have been in the early 1590s.

Finally my heartfelt thanks go to Kate Agnew who is a truly inspirational editor, and to Nigel Wheale who far away in Orkney answered a thousand questions with patience and insight.

Joshua Cross

Diane Redmond

'Greek mythology as
you have never known it:
powerfully integrated within
the weft and warp of this
fast-moving adventure
story' – Lindsey Fraser,
The Guardian

'Engaging and well-
researched' – *Times
Educational Supplement*

'Mythology for the
Playstation generation'
– *Armadillo*

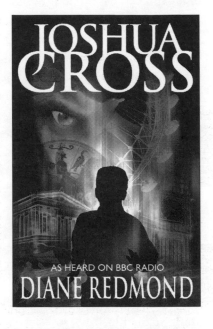

It is only when a monstrous
centaur appears from
nowhere to chase him along the Thames Embankment that
Joshua Cross becomes aware of his destiny.

Swept back in time to Ancient Greece, Josh begins an
epic journey that will lead him to the very depths of the
Underworld. But before he can return home, Josh must face
the man who destroyed his father, and who wants to kill
him, alone.

UK £4.99 • Canada $12.00 • Paperback • ISBN 1 84046 466 6

Darkness Visible: Inside the World of Philip Pullman

Nicholas Tucker

Philip Pullman is one of the world's most popular and original authors, read by children and adults alike. Containing an astonishing cast of characters, from scholarly Oxford dons to armoured bears, witches, angels, murderous Spectres and hideous harpies drawn straight from Greek mythology, Pullman's fiction can be read at many different levels.

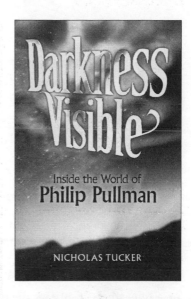

Darkness Visible looks at the world of Philip Pullman, from the flamboyant *Sally Lockhart* series and the award winning *Clockwork* and *I Was a Rat!*, to the epic *His Dark Materials* trilogy. It shows the diverse influences – from Milton and Blake to comic books and radio drama – that have shaped his writing and uncovers the part played by Pullman's unconventional childhood.

Written by acclaimed critic Nicholas Tucker, and packed with never-before-seen family photos, illustrations from Pullman's beloved graphic novels and fresh material from recent interviews, this is both a celebration of Philip Pullman and a useful guide to the rich world of his fiction.

UK £6.99 • Canada $15.00 • ISBN 1 84046 482 8

Collections of classic poetry and prose

Edited by Kate Agnew

Wizard's collections of classic poetry and prose, introduced by some of the best-loved authors for young people, are a rollercoaster ride of emotions and experience, expressed in some of the most passionate words ever written.

'Books to curl up with ... these are substantial anthologies and the choice is rich indeed. Endlessly refreshing and intriguing ... there's never a dull moment.' *Guardian*

'Wonderful ... dispels preconceptions and encourages new audiences' *Booktrusted*

'At a time when jaunty modern verse proliferates, it's good to have such well-chosen collections of poems on the most exciting subject areas of all.' Adèle Geras, *Armadillo*

'The selection and arrangement of material is brilliant, creating cross-currents, complications, and time travelling coincidences.' *Times Educational Supplement*

All royalties from these books will go to the charity National Children's Homes   the children's charity

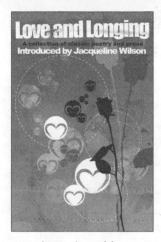

Introduced by
Jacqueline Wilson
ISBN 1 84046 523 9

Introduced by
Kevin Crossley-Holland
ISBN 1 84046 526 3

Introduced by
Philip Pullman
ISBN 1 84046 567 0

Introduced by
Michael Morpurgo
ISBN 1 84046 570 0

UK £5.99 • Canada $12.00

Big Numbers: A mind-expanding trip to infinity and back

Mary and John Gribbin
Illustrated by
Ralph Edney and
Nicholas Halliday

How big is infinity? How small is an electron?

When will the Sun destroy the Earth?

How fast is a nerve impulse in your brain?

Why can't you see inside a black hole?

What's the hottest temperature ever recorded on Earth?

What's the furthest you can see on a clear night?

Welcome to the amazing world of 'Big Numbers', where you'll travel from the furthest reaches of the known Universe to the tiniest particles that make up life on Earth. Together with Mary and John Gribbin, you can find out how our telescopes can see 10 billion years into the past, and why a thimbleful of a neutron star would contain as much mass as all the people on Earth put together!

UK £6.99 • Canada $15.00 • ISBN 1 84046 431 3

Dear Mr Morpingo: Inside the World of Michael Morpurgo

Geoff Fox

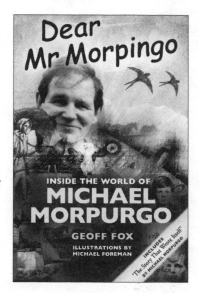

Dr Mr Morpingo

*I have just read your book
The Wreck of the Zanzibar.
It's the best book I have ever
read. It is miles better than
any Harry Potter book. BUT,
there's one thing definitely wrong
with this book. It's about a girl.
Write me a book about a boy
who gets stuck on a desert
island.*

Michael Morpurgo may be
the Children's Laureate, but
readers often have trouble spelling his name correctly. Yet
thousands and thousands of them have no trouble at all
reading stories like *The Butterfly Lion, Cool!* or *Private Peaceful.*
Or *Kensuke's Kingdom*, the best-selling story Michael wrote
about a boy stranded on a desert island to please his fan.

Dear Mr Morpingo takes you inside the world of Michael
Morpurgo to answer the questions readers love to ask –
about Michael's life, the ideas behind his stories and how
he writes.

UK £5.99 • Canada $12.00 • ISBN 1 84046 607 3